MAN
BEFORE
THE
MORNING

MAN BEFORE THE MORNING

Cecil Maiden

CHRISTIAN HERALD BOOKS
Chappaqua, New York

TO
ELIZABETH LYNNE
MY S.B.D.

PROLOGUE

The road from Joppa to Jerusalem was beset this morning by a wind that sent small, dusty eddies of red sand aswirl across the tamped earth of the caravan track. The sun had risen but an hour ago, and in the hush of early morning the movement of the three men on horseback seemed hastier than it truly was. Their haste, and the fact that they frequently turned to keep watch behind them, suggested danger.

The three had put up their simple tent last night on a rise of land between Emmaus and Lydda, though long before reaching this latter village they would turn off to the West for Arimathea. And soon they would be not only in the safety and comfort of their own homes, but Malachi, their leader, would have put the precious scrolls they

7

had brought with them from Jerusalem safely within the chest that awaited such treasures inside the synagogue at Arimathea of which he was the chief Rabbi.

Suddenly a stark figure appeared ahead of them, running over the crest of a low rocky ridge.

"It's just a boy!" the lead rider announced.

Malachi breathed a bit more easily. Even on roads as close to Jerusalem as this it was an all too common occurrence for gangs of robbers armed with clubs and swords to lie in wait for passing caravans, beat and even murder their occupants, and escape with all their goods.

Leaning forward so he could peer more intently, the second of his traveling companions said, "Yes, just a boy, apparently alone."

The men had been glad of each others' companionship on this journey—not only because of their common interest in the affairs of their synagogue, but because of the added safety they felt in each others' company on the way.

They waited in silence at his approach. But all three of them were silently relieved that the last night of the journey had passed in peace for them, and that it was good to see the small tent safely rolled and packed beside the saddle of the largest of the three horses.

By far the tallest, and for that matter the youngest of the three men, rode a little ahead of the others. Turning back to his friends, he now said, "I thought the day advanced enough for us to pass some other travelers on the road. Now I think I know why we haven't. Bandits! The boy's been hurt."

Malachi was the first to spur his horse toward the injured boy. The boy had been running, or rather staggering, across the sand, but when he saw Malachi he halted and abruptly turned about as if to run away in fear. After only a moment's hesitation, however, he turned to face the men and horses and stumbled helplessly toward them.

He was a dark-haired, handsome boy of some twelve years or so. He wore a short white tunic, and as he drew closer it was clear that his head and one of his knees was bleeding.

It seemed, however, that it was not only his physical injuries that troubled him. He was weeping silently, and Malachi, watching him closely, became aware of some sharper grief that troubled the boy. He moved his horse closer than the other two, and dismounted. And it was to Malachi that the boy now turned to speak. He pointed backward to a rise of rocky land a half mile or so away, and the words poured out of him painfully and brokenly.

"My father and my mother," he said "... our caravan of seven men and their mules..." he stopped there for a moment, gasping for breath. But the pain of what he had witnessed was only too obvious in his eyes as he faced these men.

"They've killed my father and my mother!" Tears rolled

9

down his dirt-streaked cheeks. "And all the men of our caravan, and they took all our mules with them, and the incense and the spices...."

More than that it seemed as if the boy could not find words for what was in his heart. He threw his arms out wide, convulsed by pain. It looked as if he were being stretched upon a cross. Then he fell, and Malachi caught him in his arms. Malachi spoke gently, coming to what was clearly of the greatest pain to the boy who stood there. "Your father and your mother?" he asked quietly.

The boy nodded. "I saw them ... I saw them do it!" he said, covering his eyes with one shaking hand as he spoke. "Please come with me to the place where it happened, sir. Please help me do for them ... what it is right to do!"

Malachi had drawn from the pack beside his saddle a simple linen cloth. He bandaged the boy's head and then knelt to dry the blood around his knee. He saw that he had been beaten severely for welts and bruises were everywhere on his body.

"They hurt you?" asked Malachi.

"The robbers beat and stoned me as I ran away to seek for help."

"What is your name, my son?"

"I am Joseph, sir. We came from Joppa, on our way to sell our incense to the Temple in Jerusalem, but ... please come, sir!"

MAN BEFORE THE MORNING

"Be brave, lad!" Malachi said firmly. "I'll do everything I can to help you. But here, now. Sit in my place on my horse, boy, and direct us to where it happened."

* * * *

From the sunny open courtyard of Malachi's stately home upon the outskirts of Arimathea there came a ripple of music. It was harp music, its joyful melody competing with the sound of the courtyard fountain in front of which it was being played.

A nursemaid, sitting on one of the shallow marble seats that surrounded the circular pool of the fountain, was playing the harp. And on a low, skin-draped couch near her was a little girl of about ten. She was smiling and nodding her head to the music and clasping both her hands around her knee as she did so. The nursemaid came to the end of her tune, and handed the harp across to the girl.

"It's time you tried it again, Drusilla! You know the tune quite well by now—well enough not to make any mistakes, don't you think?"

"I wish I were as patient as you are, Zuilmah! Nowadays I don't think you make any mistakes at all!"

Zuilmah gave a little smile that developed a touch of wistfulness. She looked at Drusilla with the love of an older sister. "I promised your mother that I would try to

11

teach you all the things she did so well ... harp playing, singing, even dancing!"

Drusilla glanced through the harpstrings at her nurse. It had been only a few short months since her mother had died and she still missed her sorely and tried to be all the things that her mother had wanted her to be. "This was her harp and it used to make her so happy. I know she would want me to be as happy as she used to be."

Yes, the nurse thought, her mistress had been happy, brave and cheerful even in her last illness, never thinking of herself, or of the son she had lost just two years before of the same wasting sickness. She was concerned only for her daughter and her husband.

"I think she would have laughed us out of being sad like this, just as she used to laugh my father out of his worries," Drusilla said, but she put the harp aside. She still missed her mother so keenly. "But where is Father? He should be back from Jerusalem by now, even if he called at the synagogue to store away the scrolls he went for. I think it's time we were getting ready for his return."

"Then what better way for him to see his clever girl than to find her practicing her harp for him!"

Drusilla nodded rather wryly. "I'll do my best," she said, and sat up on the couch with the harp in front of her. Then she began to play the tune that Zuilmah had been playing, a merry sort of melody that was indeed so full of happy rhythms that it was hard not to dance to it.

MAN BEFORE THE MORNING

Drusilla felt more sure of the harp and of the tune now. She threw a glance at Zuilmah which said, with a rather proud-of-it little smile, "There, now, I have remembered that tune at last. And I'm not making any mistakes any more!"

Both Drusilla and Zuilmah became immersed in the tune, and the feathery splash of the fountain just beside them seemed to add its own soft music. So absorbed in it did they become that they did not hear the sound of footsteps in the outer courtyard.

It was the cessation of these footsteps that made Drusilla look up from the harp, and what she saw at the entrance to the inner courtyard brought her quickly to her feet.

She stood there in a shaft of sunlight for a moment in amazement, then set the harp down on the couch and came forward to greet her father and the young boy whom he was carrying in his arms.

The boy was obviously in pain. He looked wonderingly at Drusilla, and despite obvious weakness, gave her a searching but warm-hearted smile. She, too, looked compassionately at him and something passed between them that had about it a sudden little thrill of mutual discovery.

Malachi lay the boy down on the couch by the fountain and reached out to embrace his daughter and lifted her joyfully in his arms as he did so.

"This is Joseph," he said. "And we must do all we can for

him, Drusilla. Zuilmah, quickly now, wash his wounds and pour some oil onto them."

Zuilmah was already on her feet, waiting there for orders. "I'll bring a pitcher of water and some olive oil. I have some soft, fresh linen to bind his wounds until he's well again."

Malachi nodded his approval. "Hurry back, Zuilmah; Drusilla will stay here with him and do whatever she can do to help, too."

"Yes, Master." Zuilmah hurried away towards a door at the other side of the courtyard. And Drusilla went over to Joseph and supported him with her own slender arm. She sensed by his eyes and her father's reticence that his wounds were deeper than these that showed. She smiled at him sympathetically. "Nobody in our house is as good as Zuilmah at things like this. And I will help her, too, Joseph."

"Thank you. You and your father are kind."

Drusilla smiled at him and Malachi, watching her making the boy comfortable, turned away and went into his own bed-chamber, opening and closing a door that was quite near to them. He was tired from his long journey, from the responsibility of working for the synagogue, from this ordeal on the road . . . yes, maybe of life itself. He was a silent man, who did not wear his sorrow openly. But since his wife's death, despair was his close companion. Yet now his heart was moved by this boy's tragedy.

Once inside his room Malachi walked toward a patch of

sunlight in the window. There he bowed his head in prayer
. . . seeking an answer to a question that had been burdening him.

"O Lord Jehovah!" he prayed silently, "Since for so many months my child, Drusilla, has been left without a mother—and there be none left to her in this family save only thy servant, Malachi, show me, O Lord, if it be right for me, should Joseph indeed have no kinsfolk, as he did tell me on the way here, show me if it be right for me to bid him live here in this house . . . bringing to Drusilla all the comfort and the joy of having a brother again . . . and I . . . a son."

After a few short moments Malachi opened his eyes again. He felt as he stood there that indeed the Lord looked with special favor on his plea. And the sunshine around him seemed all the brighter because of his new hope. He felt, as fathers sometimes do, the great, wide surge of time and the quickening drift of the years.

CHAPTER
1

Twenty years had come and gone since the boy Joseph had first set foot in the house of Malachi at Arimathea. And of all the events that had occurred in this house since then, few had had about them more urgency than what was happening this day.

The secret of that urgency lay beyond the door that had just closed upon Joseph and his father Malachi. It was a massive wooden door, and no sound came from beyond it now.

Malachi and Joseph continued to stare at the closed portal. And for the moment they stood in an almost tangible silence as those do who stand at a graveside. Sadness seemed to hang like an invisible veil over things—over the marble and cedar of the courtyard, over the new spring leaves in the fig trees, over the feathery drift of the fountain and the flutter of the turtle doves around the eaves. Even the distance seemed to wait, as if silence and sadness stretched far on and out across the fields toward the wildflowers on the slopes of the twin peaks about whose feet spread Arimathea itself.

After some moments of staring at the closed door, Malachi turned to look yet again at the muscular young man who was both foster son and son-in-law to him. Joseph now sat five or six yards away on the other side of the fountain.

They had come to mean much to each other, these two, even though now and then there erupted differences of opinion and attitude to the Romans, to the rules of the Sanhedrin, even to so many aspects of daily life itself.

Little had Malachi thought, when he took that young boy into his home, that he would be not only a son to him, one to take the place of his son who had died, but also a fitting husband for his beloved daughter Drusilla. At first he had not agreed to the marriage. It seemed wrong. None of them, he thought, would be able to tolerate the change of affections and positions. But gradually he came to see that their happiness depended on it. They had grown in love and wisdom and were devoted to one another. Finally he gave his consent, and he saw their lives blossom . . . until now. And now Drusilla might, on this disturbing day, be in mortal danger from the same wasting sickness that had taken his other loved ones from him.

MAN BEFORE THE MORNING

Malachi glanced across at the closed door again, wondering what his friend Sosthenes, one of the best of the Greek physicians in Jerusalem, was at this very moment discovering beyond that door that remained so frighteningly closed.

He forced himself to think more positive thoughts about his daughter. He reflected on the golden years of her growing up.

Glancing across at Joseph again, Malachi was a little startled to see a man of thirty-two looking at him—it was a face that demonstrated courage yet also asked for support, hope and consolation. It was a totally familiar face, one that only occasionally suggested the lost, orphaned child. It was the face of a strong and principled man who was yet afflicted with some inner longing.

Malachi broke the silence.

"Whatever Sosthenes may discover in there," he said, "you may be sure he'll know what's best to do about it. He has the wisdom of the better Greek physicians, Joseph, plus a sense of humor."

The older man's voice had reassurance in it, the kind of reassurance for which Joseph had been mutely asking. But it also had the curious ring of detachment that Joseph so often found exasperating. As he looked at his father this afternoon he realized once again that Malachi looked almost as Greek as the physician to whom he was referring.

Sitting as still as he was, Joseph thought that the folds of the purple himation Malachi was wearing gave him the kind of sculptured dignity that must, he supposed, be more familiar in Athens than in Jerusalem. Perhaps the wiry, steel-gray curls had something to do with this, for even though Malachi was but fifty-five, his hair was almost entirely gray.

"Let's see that we don't lose ours, Joseph," Malachi added.

"Our what, Father?"

"Our sense of humor. Your mind's far away, son, isn't it?"

Joseph glanced back at him. "Where else could it be but in there?" he said, motioning to the room behind him.

Malachi smiled, and there was more warmth and sympathy in the smile now.

Joseph saw that his foster father was trying to ease the strain of waiting, and he realized that he too must do anything he could to make things seem a little easier. He must try for instance not to think any more of that closed door until it opened. He must make an effort to talk about something else. Almost any kind of talk would be better than this measuring of moments. It was ironic, he thought, that he had been brought to this household a victim, but he had become a survivor. Now his dearest love who had guided him back to life was herself a victim of a dread disease and perhaps facing death.

He pulled himself together. "A few minutes ago," he said "while Sosthenes was waiting out here for Zuilmah to get

MAN BEFORE THE MORNING

Drusilla ready for this examination, he was trying to keep my spirits up by laughing at the 'battle of the egg' that's broken out again. He spoke as if it were the first time he'd heard of it."

"Not that old argument again!"

"He was asking how so many grown-up men could take so long deliberating among themselves as to what, if some heretical hen were lawless enough to lay an egg on the Sabbath, should be done with the egg? With all those rabbis of Shammai's persuasion saying that to eat it would be to profane the Sabbath, and Hillel's noisy crowd declaring 'Eat it and give thanks!' Poor Sosthenes! I'm afraid that such solemnity on such a point must be beyond him. And I wonder what you'd say, Father?"

"That the Pharisees should have something better in their cluttered heads to worry about."

There was the expected touch of contempt in Malachi's voice. It was still impossible for his foster father to raise an honest laugh about the Pharisees. He could, as usual, only smile and condescend, as so many of his fellow Sadducees were wont to do. In fact Joseph realized that condescension might almost be looked upon as a Sadducean characteristic.

He got restlessly to his feet, putting one sandaled foot on the rim of the marble basin of the fountain. And he stared down at his own reflection, broken, now, into a thousand shimmering images where the spray of the

21

fountain blew across the face of the water.

Something about that broken image in the fountain appealed to Joseph's sense of congruity—as if its agitation were a reproduction of his own mental state. It bothered him, though, to realize that he looked so peculiarly boyish. At thirty-two a man should have more physical dignity about him. After all, he asked himself, was he not already one of the most qualified of the new scribes recently admitted to the great Sanhedrin?

He was wearing a brown tunic, and from where he was standing over the fountain pond he could see the reflection of his muscular legs to a point above his knees. The bright sunlight highlighted the folds of his tunic, his face and the rough dark curls above it.

Malachi's voice cut across his restlessness: "The Pharisees might well be more amusing, Joseph, if their schemes were not becoming so insidious."

"Not only insidious, Father, but dangerous. And there are enough of them in the Sanhedrin now to out-vote you on almost anything you might think about."

"Not while your Uncle Caiaphas is there to overrule them! They still don't question the authority of the High Priest, my son."

Joseph paced restlessly along the rim of the fountain.

"Authority? Why do we still go shouting up and down Jerusalem about authority? It hasn't got much meaning any more. Authority! Where did Pilate find authority for dipping into the Temple treasury again to build this newest aqueduct of his!"

"That's an entirely different matter."

"It's only a different matter because convenience makes it so. It's obviously not a question of what's right or wrong in the Council on such matters, but rather a question of what is there to be gotten out of it? Have you heard of the prices some of your under treasurers have been getting lately for the sale of special privileges?"

Malachi looked sharply at his son-in-law. "The sale of special privileges?"

"You can't be ignorant of it any longer, Father. Since I returned from my journey round the synagogues in Galilee, I've learned what a Sanhedrin lawyer is supposed to wink at."

"You're forgetting yourself, Joseph! This worry about Drusilla's gone to your head."

"Not enough to blind me to the things that have been going on right at my feet. Surely in my own home I can talk freely of them?"

"Of course you can."

"Well, one thing I've learned, Father, is that avarice is no respector of persons. It can manipulate a Sadducee just as easily as it can manipulate a Pharisee. And the danger's growing so fast that soon. . . ."

"Joseph!" It was not Malachi's voice this time.

Joseph swung round to see that the physician Sosthenes was coming through the door at last.

In the few seconds that elapsed before he reached them, Joseph also caught a glimpse of Zuilmah, who had been nursemaid to Drusilla since her childhood. Zuilmah came hurrying out of the room with a troubled look on her face. In her hand was a towel that the doctor had used. She closed the door and moved quickly away toward the kitchen quarters.

Sosthenes put a comforting hand on Joseph's shoulder, and the physician's kindly, aristocratic face was full of understanding.

"The wasting sickness has gone too far now for us to have any hope of arresting it, Joseph. I don't think there's actually much pain—except when she's coughing. But she's very weak. And for all her courage there's probably a kind of constant, underlying ache that must be very wearying."

Malachi had risen and come close to them.

"I want you to be very frank with us, Sosthenes," he said, and after searching the doctor's face with unaccustomed hesitation, he added, "How long do you suppose...?"

Fighting the surge of fear that rose in him, Joseph heard his own voice echoing the words. "How long?" he asked.

"You can't expect to have her with you many weeks longer."

MAN BEFORE THE MORNING

Joseph turned sharply away from the old physician, and though his gaze fell over Malachi's shoulder toward the hills, he was but little aware of what he saw there. He did not notice that the sun was lower in the sky, or that the wind was rising and the grasses were rippling in the fields.

"What can we do for her?" he heard Malachi ask. He turned to see that his foster father's face was gray with resignation, with a kind of shocked acceptance of something he had been refusing to acknowledge for a long time—the reoccurrence of this family curse.

"Let her sleep," Sosthenes said. "Sleep is what is best for her, and freedom from disturbance for both mind and body. And more of the same good goat's milk and barley porridge—whenever she can eat it."

Joseph asked quietly, "Does she know . . . Sosthenes? Does she know you feel there isn't any hope of recovery?"

Sosthenes shook his head with a faint, grave smile of understanding pity. "Let's not risk shortening such a time as you have left with her, Joseph, by any cause for grieving. If she were told I fear she might just fold her hands and quietly accept it—and simply slip away from us."

"Accept it? Not Drusilla! Oh Sosthenes, I must go in and talk with her."

"She's waiting for you. And Malachi, she thinks you're still in Jerusalem. It would be better, I think, if we could act as if there'd not been any urgency to summon you here from the Council."

Malachi looked toward the inner room for a long moment, and then: "I would not have her troubled," he said quietly. "I would not even have her puzzled, Sosthenes. I'll go back to Jerusalem with you, if I may."

"I'd be grateful for your company, old friend."

Malachi turned to his adopted son before he left. "You've never shirked things, Joseph. Never since the day I first set eyes on you on that road outside Lydda. You were just a twelve-year-old then. You always possessed a lot of courage. I don't think you've ever lost any of it."

For a moment Joseph rested his hand on the older man's shoulder, briefly nodding his understanding. Then he turned, and gently opening the door, went in at last to Drusilla.

She was lying back on her pillows at the head of the low bed by the windows, but when she saw him she raised herself on an elbow, leaning eagerly forward. Her soft black hair fell freely about her shoulders. The sun was behind her now, touching the outline of her head in an edge of gold that threw the rest of her face into soft shadow.

"Poor Joseph!" she said, "Sosthenes kept you waiting out there such a long time. He likes to be sure about everything. What did he tell you?"

"To make sure you ate your porridge."

MAN BEFORE THE MORNING

She laughed a little at that. "You're beginning to treat me as if I were a five-year-old!"

He came forward and sat on the fur rug at her bedside, pressing her thin hands between his own. She lay back on the pillows again, smiling contentedly.

"Five-year-olds have little to worry about!" he said.

"But I'm not so far from thirty!"

"And an 'old married woman,' as you sometimes say! I'll have to love those extra years away from you again!" Her eyes smiled gratefully, and he leaned forward and kissed her on the brow.

She said, "He told me I must try to sleep a little more. He said I must only get out of bed when there's someone here to help me."

"That's very sensible. And surely Zuilmah must be at your side when I'm away."

She nodded, but turned the talk to something closer to her heart. "I'm getting tired of not being useful, Joseph. I want to be up and doing. There's so much I ought to be doing."

"You've always been an active little rebel, Drusilla. Let's give Sosthenes his way for a while."

After a moment she nodded reluctantly. "I suppose his way's the only way I'll ever be permitted to get out and about again. But now of all times—with Passover only a week away! I wanted to go up to Jerusalem with you, and into the Temple with the others."

"But I shall be here with you—as much and as often as I can. Starting today. I'll be right here beside you, here in Arimathea. In fact I shall be home not only through tomorrow, until the Sabbath ends, but I've been excused attendance in the Temple the day after, too! And after that I will be beside you just as many hours as I can get away."

"Bless you, my husband! But don't take any risks about offending them." She studied him more closely, then added,

"There's something I've been worrying about."

"To do with the Sanhedrin?"

She nodded, looking at him with a new anxiety.

"Last week," she said, "when Uncle Caiaphas came to see me, I was telling him how well they had received you in those synagogues in Galilee. I told him that he must have realized before he sent you on that mission how much respect you would command there."

Joseph shook his head. "I don't think that would overly impress him. What did he say?"

"He made a dismal face about it," she broke into a cheerful laugh at the memory. "After all, he wouldn't need to change his face very much to look a little dismal now and then would he? Anyway, he said rather pointedly that he'd yet to find you winning much respect in Jerusalem. He told me that he thinks you've lost much of your spirit. Nowadays, he said, you usually sit there in that weighty semicircle with a scowl on your face. He says you only speak when spoken to."

28

MAN BEFORE THE MORNING

But Joseph was looking fondly at her again, barely hearing the words she had just said to him. He closed his firm hand over her arm and said, "I am twice blessed, beloved. Blessed as a brother would be, then blessed as your husband."

She looked up into his face with a deep brightness in her eyes. "I think that God was good to both of us, Joseph. I little thought all those years ago when Father brought you in from that awful tragedy on the Lydda road that the boy whose wounds dear Zuilmah and I were tending that day would fall in love with me ten years later, and make me fall in love with him!"

He stooped to kiss her. "So I made you fall in love with me!" He even managed to laugh a little.

"Of course you did! You always make people do as you want. Even to giving you that job as a junior scribe, the job that led you even into the great Sanhedrin."

She stopped there, sounding a little exhausted—so much so that he smoothed the pillow on which she was lying and lifted her very tenderly a little higher in her bed.

"I complain too much about my work, so just forget," he told her, "what I've said to you about being shouted down in the Sanhedrin. They talk such rubbish there, my beloved! Certainly not much that's fit for a devoted wife to hear!"

Joseph glanced away from her and stared through the window. "It wasn't like that to begin with," he declared. "I soon discovered that they're scared to death of anybody blunt enough to point out all their contradictions and hypocrisies! So they take a weak man's line and try to shout their own way out of things. If you'd been shouted down as often as I. . . ." He stopped there, remembering her condition.

Drusilla hesitated, then spoke more gently. "If I know my Joseph—and I ought to, having been a sister to him years before love obscured his faults—I know he is forthright and not easily put down." She gave him a smile that told him how grateful she was for his nearness, and then: "Has Zibeon been bothering you again?"

"Not directly. I think he's biding his time, Drusilla. But let's talk of chasing all those shadows out of your eyes!"

"I know a way of getting rid of them."

"How?"

"Joseph! Dear Joseph! Don't you ever stop to think how your stay-at-home wife must feel about these things now and then? I don't want Father and Uncle Caiaphas to think of you as just another thorn in the Sanhedrin's side. From all accounts there are too many already. And we all worked so hard to get you into it! Nor do I want to hear about you sitting still there, full of smothered protests. You could be up and leading them! That's what my husband is meant to do!"

He touched his lips to her fingertips and was shocked to find how cold they were. He tried to push away the sudden fear that rose in him. He could no more have told her now of the conflict in his heart—his sharpening scorn for all the cant that was going on around him in the Sanhedrin—than he could have told her what Sosthenes had just said. Then the sudden, sickening realization beat down on him that within a few short weeks it might not matter what Drusilla thought of all his lack of action.

"I've always been so proud of you!" she was saying. "When I'm strong enough to go back into Jerusalem with you, I want them to watch me striding beside you, and I want to hear them whispering to one another, after we've gone by, "That's Joseph, you know, Joseph of Arimathea, the one who's turning the tide and bringing back the great days once again!"

"Dear love!" he said, "What would you have me do, I wonder?"

"I think the thing to ask is not so much what I would have you do, Joseph, as to find out what is going on inside the head of Uncle Caiaphas."

"What do you mean?"

"He said that if the things I tried to tell him about you were the truth, then he'd have to find some way of seeing that you didn't hide your light beneath a bushel any more. I think he's going to make some kind of test for you."

"That sounds like Caiaphas all right! A pity he can't find some way to test himself, Drusilla. What sort of thing do you suppose he has in mind?"

"I think he's going to send you on some special errand—something to do with the fuss and bother about that man from Galilee."

"You mean the Nazarene?"

Drusilla nodded. "They say such crowds are following him these days that he could be a danger to the lot of us."

"I wonder."

The unfamiliar sharpness in his voice made her look up at him with curiosity.

"What do you wonder?"

He parried the question. "Has Zuilmah brought in any further tales about him lately? Did you hear what people have been swearing happened up in Bethany?"

"No—what was it?"

"There is a man there called Lazarus. They say this Jesus raised him from the dead!"

"But that's preposterous! They must have faked his death."

"That's not what Nicodemus says, and he appears to know more than the rest about it. He says this Lazarus had been buried for four days before it happened!"

"How can he believe such a tale? It must be very comforting to be a Pharisee and feel so sure there is a resurrection from the dead."

"The Pharisees are not the only ones who think that way."

"There's nothing in the Torah. . . ."

"How like your father's daughter!" he exclaimed, and

instantly regretted the edge of criticism in his voice. "I'm sorry, my dear love! It's just that—well, you know how much your father and I can differ in these things."

"He loves you very dearly, Joseph. And you must remember that what he believes is what he learned at his father's knee. It is what all the men closest to us have been taught all the way back to Zadok the Priest, I suppose. It troubles me that all these years there's been this wall between you. And every year the two of you appear to build it higher."

"The only wall that separates him from me is the very real wall he walks behind each day, Drusilla—the Temple wall. And as Chief Treasurer he is so busy counting shekels and intoning words above them that he cannot even hear the murmuring of the people. All the blood of sheep and goats in those sacrifices is as nothing to the way in which the people, the ordinary people with whom he never mixes, are being bled by...."

Drusilla had paled a little as she listened, and suddenly a fit of coughing seized her. It shook her small frame violently and in the grip of it she groped spasmodically for the towel at her bedside. When he gave it to her, there were tears of shame in his eyes.

"Forgive me, Drusilla! I get so caught up in these things."

While the fit of coughing spent itself, he clasped his hands together so tightly that the intertwined, long fingers drained, began shaking and turned white.

After a while the coughing was over, though, and she lay exhausted on the pillow again.

"I wonder if you know," he said, "how beautiful your hair looks when it's loose around your head like that!"

She smiled but did not speak.

"When you were a little girl, Drusilla, and I'd been rescued and brought home to live with you...."

"You used to pull my hair!" She tried to laugh at him.

"You used to deserve it! But that wasn't what I was thinking about. I was remembering that one fine day I made a crown of wild anemones for you. You had a little wooden doll in those days—the one with the painted face. And we made a cradle of rushes for him, and you said he was Moses, and you, of course, were Pharaoh's daughter."

She remembered.

"And we floated him off in his cradle," she said, "until the river took him so far away that you had to run right down the hill after him. Those were the happy days, Joseph! Those were the happy days! The anemones must be starting to come out again by now, don't you think? Later in the spring we'll walk up there and see if that bend in the river looks just as it used to look."

"Later in the spring," he said.

"That is," and she laughed at last, "if I remember to eat my porridge, I suppose!"

"If you eat your porridge," he said.

CHAPTER
2

From the lighting of the Sabbath lamp to the sound of the trumpet that proclaimed the Sabbath's end—the trumpet from the roof of the synagogue at the other end of the village—Joseph had hardly left Drusilla's side.

In addition to his frightening new awareness of her sickness, another great uneasiness had been growing in him, but he had not spoken of it. They would live one day at a time, and each new day was a reward and a blessing. He had decided that he would not share his shadows, but give whatever peace and light he could to her. He had vowed, since listening to Sosthenes, that he would crowd into whatever days remained as much real joy and true happiness for her as he could steal from the future that had once seemed to stretch so promisingly out in front of them.

Yet hers, he had discovered, was now a little world, bound physically by the shapes and colors of the few familiar objects in the room around her, by the view from her window and by the shadows on the wall.

The sun shone all day long for the two of them. And he had found, sitting on the low bed and cushioning her head against his shoulder, that she too had come to realize the shrinking of the world that she could share with him.

It was a world of very simple experiences: of comical patterns in the olive trees, of moments when the butterflies would sit in sudden-frozen stillness on the sprays of tamarisk near the window, of watching fledglings learning how to fly, or lying back to listen to the sounds of the far courtyard fountain.

For a short time during the morning of the next day, the Sabbath, she had felt jubilant enough to call to Zuilmah for her harp, and for a spell they had sung together. Joseph had kept down his own deep voice so that her weaker one could wind around and soar above it. She had not been able to do this very long, though, for the spells of coughing had put an end to the brief music.

Zuilmah had made for her mistress on the previous day a confection of honey-paste flavored with jasmine, one of Drusilla's favorite sweetmeats.

There were fresh dates, brought over the hills from Jericho within the last few days by Joseph's white-haired steward, Jubal, who had been permitted to visit a daughter there. And there were the new season's figs, full and juicy with the bloom of spring on them.

Drusilla had slept quite often through the day, seeming to tire quite suddenly only to wake again a little later refreshed and full of plans for changes in the house or in her garden.

She had chatted on with an animation to match her eagerness. But there had been no further talk of the Sanhedrin. Nor had there been any mention of Caiaphas, the brother of Drusilla's gentle mother. It seemed as if she and Joseph had made a wordless pact that they would not discuss any subject which could bring disappointment or ire to the day of rest.

But the sun sank down at last and at the sound of the distant trumpet, it was Joseph himself who brought to his wife the basin of fresh water in which they washed their hands. Then they poured wine into two goblets which they held together giving thanks for the day according to the Law.

Soon afterwards Drusilla told him she needed to sleep. He held her closely, and she clung to him quite tightly with her thin, cold arms.

Finally, he smoothed the pillow underneath her head, and kissed her brow again. He was tired, too, worn by the strain. A couch had been moved into the room for him. For another moment or so he stood at the open window, gazing at the glitter of the stars.

At length he turned to look at her again. She was already asleep.

"The Lord bless thee and keep thee," he whispered. "The Lord make his face shine upon thee, and be gracious unto thee. The Lord lift up his countenance upon thee, and give thee peace."

After that he too lay down. And though for quite a time his eyes were open in the darkness, he at length fell fast asleep.

* * * *

The next day was the one in which he had been excused from his duties in the Temple. Yet the moment Joseph heard his steward's knock upon the door, he knew in his heart that the apprehension that he had thrust to the back of his mind throughout the Sabbath had dawned upon him, and that somewhere, somehow, danger threatened.

"What is it, Jubal?"

"There's a messenger here, sir, from the Sanhedrin." The old man kept his voice down in deference to the sleeping Drusilla.

"Tell him to wait in the atrium. I'll come out to him."

"I'll tell him, sir."

Joseph threw back the light fur rug that covered him, and swung his legs off the couch as he did so. He took his cloak from the top of the chest where he had laid it, and as quietly as possible, opened the door and closed it behind him as he went into the atrium beyond.

The messenger was standing on the other side of the fountain. Joseph was glad to see that they had sent Matthias, for he was the youngest of the messengers, and probably the most agreeable.

The youth in the short brown tunic raised an arm in salutation and bowed respectfully.

Joseph acknowledged the salutation as he strode forward. "What brings you here so early, Matthias? It must have been still dark in Jerusalem when you left."

"It was, my lord Joseph. But the Suffragan summons you to an urgent meeting."

"When?"

"As soon as you can get there."

"The Council—or all of them?"

"The full Sanhedrin, sir."

"Did the Suffragan explain that I was excused—but I won't embarrass you, lad. Besides, by this time you must be hungry, even though you may have eaten before you came. Go into the kitchen, Matthias, and tell them to give you some food. I'll wash and be ready for the journey. Tell them I'll eat now, too."

"Yes, sir."

Back in the sleeping room he washed in the bowl of water Jubal had already brought there, then hurriedly gathered his coat and sandals. Joseph looked at Drusilla as she slept, longing to talk to her yet making up his mind not to wake her since her breathing seemed less troubled now.

He left word with Jubal for Drusilla, promising to hurry back. Then with Matthias keeping his donkey just a neck behind that of Joseph, the two of them were out on the country road together hurrying south towards Jerusalem.

The day was clear and bright and over the upland meadows a wind was blowing. Already there was a touch of warmth in the wind, and the scents of spring were in it.

Others were also on the road early, and, though the Passover was still five days away, some groups of travelers, singing as they came, were clearly pilgrims. They went joyfully on their way hoping to reach Jerusalem in time to share with friends and kinsfolk the gossip and excitement of the days before the holiday.

The youth Matthias, as befitted a messenger in the company of such a personage as a Councillor of the Sanhedrin, would only speak when spoken to. But Joseph's genuine interest in the youth soon ended such an artificial silence.

"You're looking pleased and excited this morning, Matthias," Joseph said cheerfully. "What are you thinking about?"

"An egg," said Matthias.

"Why an egg?"

"I ate one, sir. They gave me an egg to eat in your house."

Joseph's raised eyebrows and obvious astonishment prompted him to add, "Not that I haven't eaten the egg of a hen before, sir. My cousin brought some down from Bethel one day in the winter."

"And I shall bring you more, Matthias. Remind me!" Joseph looked at the lad with wonder, face to face again with the distance placed between himself and such young men by his wealth, and the way of life born of that wealth. But he also remembered himself at that age—how vulnerable he felt.

"Tell me about your family, Matthias."

Matthias in his turn betrayed surprise. It was seldom that a Sadducee showed any interest in such things.

"There are but four of us left, sir. The married ones are all away. There are my father and mother and my small brother Reuben and me."

"How does your father earn his living?"

"He was a potter, sir—a very good one. But the palsy has taken him so badly that his hands can't turn his wheel these days. Half the time he's in such pain that it's hard for us to move him. My mother earns a little extra now and then by helping Simeon the sandal-maker, and Reuben earns a few mites more by carrying water. He's very little, so he can carry little, and he spills it. It's mostly what I earn as a messenger that keeps us going. There was trouble last week with a moneylender. You see, sir, with the Roman taxes...."

"The Roman taxes!"

Matthias wondered at the sharpness in the voice of Joseph. "There's more real hardship in Judea because of these taxes, Matthias, than there's ever been. But that's a subject..." Joseph broke off abruptly. One did not speak of politics to a Sanhedrin messenger.

"Only the very rich," said Matthias with quick bitterness, "can find a safe way of avoiding them!" And he realized immediately that he was speaking to one of the wealthiest men in the Sanhedrin. He felt the blood rise to his cheeks, and fell to silence once again, letting his donkey lag still further behind that of the Councillor, determined not to fall into some further trap of words.

From both sides of the tamped-earth road that ran along the top of the hills there came the stimulating, slightly pungent smell of brushwood, mixed here and there with a sharper scent from the waving billows of wild mustard. And as the road approached Jerusalem, absorbing the highway that wound in from the West— from Gibeon and far off Joppa—the way grew thick with pilgrims for the Passover.

With them were traveling merchants and itinerant peddlers, some with a string of camels, the humbler ones with nimble-footed asses. They were laden with silks and linens, purple cloths from Tyre and Sidon, veils and sandals, scents and spices, trinkets and masses of small jewelry that must arrive in Jerusalem early enough to sell to all and sundry through the holiday.

The highway rose above the brow of a hill, then fell toward the small pool of Bethesda. On either side, some of them already occupied, were low *succoths*, the tents in which so many thousands of the annual pilgrims (especially those who had no relatives within the city) would spend the days between now and the feast itself.

From here the Holy City rose in front of them, its crowded mesh of narrow streets, its houses, halls and palaces reaching ever up toward the gleaming gold and white Temple itself. It was a teeming miracle in brass and bronze, and the smoke of its great altar fire was already wreathing its gray-brown awesomeness into the morning sky.

So clear was the air on this spring morning that above the rumble of traffic in the streets, above the wheels of the carts and an occasional Roman chariot, it was possible to hear, though thin and distant, the chanting of the Levites in the court of the Priests up there. It was a solemn sound, drawing its minor melodies from far across the centuries of Jewish history.

Beyond the Fish Gate it was so crowded now that it was no longer possible to ride, and Joseph dismounted, and Matthias, still troubled by his awkward shyness, dismounted too, coming forward to take both beasts and lead them off to where all other animals belonging to officials of the Temple would be tethered for the day.

"Remind me about those eggs!" cried Joseph after him. And more at his ease, Matthias smiled back at him. He raised an arm in leave-taking, then bowed and was soon lost among the crowd.

By the time Joseph had hurried up the many steps and come through the people in the Court of the Gentiles, and had finally been admitted by the Temple guard into the Chamber of Hewn Stone, the meeting of the Great Sanhedrin was already in progress.

So sharp was the air of crisis that as he made his way along the upper semicircle of stone benches to his place among the twelve men of the Council, he got little more than a brief nod of recognition from the High Priest in the center. He did, however, notice how tensely Malachi, his foster father, was leaning forward in his place on the other side of the semicircle.

One of the fifty-nine members of the Sanhedrin who did not belong to the high Council was standing at his seat on the lower floor, addressing the others rather wildly. He was a timid yet blustering Pharisee whom Joseph knew of old, a man called Dathan of Bethphage. And as he looked around at the faces of the others, the agitated man seemed to gather himself together as if for an ultimatum.

"It's a wonder to me this matter hasn't come to a head before," he said. "There's not a man here who hasn't known that sooner or later the whole Sanhedrin would have to bring it out into the open and meet the threat together, once and for all. What are your wishes, Caiaphas?"

The High Priest rose and took a step or two toward the edge of the raised stone platform. As he did so a silence fell so completely that it was possible to hear the thin, small tinkle of the bells on the hem of his robe.

For a second or two he simply stared at them, with a forward thrust of his bearded chin and a lift of his head that seemed to hold them captive there beneath him.

He was a lean and swarthy man, this Caiaphas, well in his middle years. His leanness was offset by a predatory crouching of the shoulders. But the embroidered *meil*, the robe of the ephod, was straight enough to counteract the stoop. And his voice was sharp and penetrating.

Today his words rang with a curious mixture of incompatibles—a blend, it might appear, of apprehension and relief. The fear was unfamiliar. His relief might well have sprung from the fact that now at last there was to be a settling of the matter that had long worried him.

"It's quite a challenge that this thing has happened in the week of Passover. But to those of you who've watched this Nazarene as I have, it's hardly unexpected. In fact it's obvious that he picked this week. He picked it so that he might inflame the biggest crowd he could reach!"

Caiaphas abruptly swung his eyes toward Joseph, giving him another nod of recognition. Then he turned back to the others.

"Masters," he said, "our Councillor from Arimathea has only just arrived. I'll ask the Suffragan to tell him what's been going on here in Jerusalem. Joseph, the Suffragan was witness to it. Tell him, Mordecai."

The tall, white-bearded Suffragan rose from his place at Caiaphas' side. "My lord," he said, turning to Joseph but including the assembly in what he said, "when I was on my way into the Temple, the crowds out beyond the Sheep Gate were thicker than I've ever seen them! They must have known this Nazarene was coming. There was a line of them that stretched right out to the end of the road from Olivet."

A voice called out, "Behaving just as if they waited for a king!"

Mordecai ignored the comment. "When this Jesus came in sight there was a surge toward him. He was sitting on a colt, I think, and it looked as if some of his followers had thrown some of their clothes across it. I couldn't see too closely—I was quite a distance off. He didn't look particularly dangerous, though."

Mordecai spoke quietly. He was obviously not the type of man to stoop to any wild embroidery of his tale. Yet like so many other Sadducees embarked on such a theme, he had the knack of making it appear as if it were the doings of some slave he was describing.

"Nor did his followers impress me," he went on. "But what would you expect? Wretched nonentities from Galilee! Unlettered fishermen, peasants, even a tax collector, I've been told are his followers. They're a commonplace lot, though not on the whole fanatical."

One of the listeners below the platform, a wiry, gaunt muscular man, was quick to fasten on the word.

"Fanatical? Isn't it fanatical, then, for this Nazarene to say he would *destroy* the Temple and build it in three days again?"

The measured voice of Joseph's foster father, Malachi, countered the question sharply. "Hardly fanatical, Jacob. More imbecilic, I'd say."

The Suffragan looked at his audience and continued.

"The crowds grew thicker every moment. They left the booths and tents they were building for themselves outside the gates and turned the thing into quite a progress. They even strewed their garments on the road in front of him!"

"As if he were a king!" called the same voice as before.

"They cut down branches from the palm trees," went on Mordecai, "carpeting his way with them or waving them and dipping them in front of him until it looked as if a frenzy had possessed them."

"And *that*, Masters," Caiaphas cried, "That's where the danger lies! Not in this Nazarene's deceptive, meek appearance. Not in that straggle of ignorant men who followed him from Galilee. The danger's in his power to turn this multitude into a mob!"

In the brief pause needed to let the words sink in, Mordecai looked at them triumphantly. Then he concluded what he had to say. "After that," he went on—and he was speaking loudly now—"they all began to shout him on his way. 'Hosanna!' they yelled after him. 'Blessed be the kingdom of our father David!' 'Blessed be the King that cometh in the name of the Lord!' "

The watching faces were growing angry.

"They called him 'King' then? And did he let them call him King?"

"Merciful Heaven! I hope there weren't too many Romans within earshot."

"When is there not a Roman within earshot, Caleb? Be realistic! Up there in the Antonia guardhouse they will already be inventing more of their foul-mouthed jokes about it. They'll be laughing their ugly heads off. At whom, do you suppose?"

"At the Sanhedrin?"

"Who else!"

"Better to laugh behind their walls than march down here again."

Another Pharisaic voice, pungent with sarcasm, cried, "The Legions will stay well beyond the Temple courts awhile, even though the cost of flattering them to keep their distance is rising so alarmingly."

Caiaphas put an end to this. "Masters! This is not the outskirts of the Sheep Gate!" He paused and glared, and then went on, "Our friend from Arimathea has still learned but the half of it. There's something else, Joseph, something that happened but an hour ago. Not all the members of this gathering know about it yet. I'll have our good friend Zibeon ben Gorah tell you of it."

The agitated murmur died again, but did so fitfully.

One of the younger scribes rose to his feet in the body of the hall, lifting the fold of his brown tunic a little as he did so. He was a handsome, muscular man of roughly Joseph's age, tall in build and broad of shoulder. There was a Grecian look about him—tight brown curls outlined his impressive head, and his mouth had a fine, classic appearance. But his light blue eyes held treachery, shifting from one side to the other. They were cruel eyes, aglint with some peculiar, sensual ferocity that was in keeping with the upturn of his chin.

His voice was smooth and confident, yet it was curiously furtive.

"This Jesus came into the outer court with quite a crowd behind him. The place was pretty full already, and there were many women there. Children too for that matter. But any who saw him make his entrance must have realized from the way he stood in the midst there, staring angrily about him, that he was looking for trouble."

"Did you hear what he had to say to them?"

"He threw the words of the prophets at them. He told them it was written that this house should be a house of prayer. He told them that they were making it a den of thieves!"

Caiaphas sat in stony silence, knowing well the reason for the smothered trace—the quickly-smothered trace —of bitter laughter that was directed from the body of the hall at him. For not a man there failed to realize that as Keeper of the Law and the Prophets he could scarcely voice a protest at such a clear allusion to them.

Malachi came to the High Priest's rescue. "This Nazarene has shown before how well he knows the prophets, but what Esaias said is no authority for a rabble rouser to take the law into his own hands."

Caiaphas threw him a grateful nod, breathing more freely. "One tongue," he commented aside, "would not be apt to do much damage if it were not for the many thousands of other tongues that ache to echo its words! More of them every moment so it seems."

The High Priest turned to the body of the hall again. "Tell us what happened next, Zibeon."

Zibeon nodded, making the most of the attention he was getting. "Next he started fighting with those selling in the courtyard. His scourge lashed out at all who came in reach of it. And a pretty mess he made of the money tables! For all I know the changers may still be down on their hands and knees, trying to salvage as many shekels as they can. The sheep and goats panicked on the spot, kicking tables in all directions. And how do you suppose the followers of the Nazarene behaved? They *praised* him for it! That might not have mattered so much if the crowd had not taken up the chant. Even the children. Some of them called 'Hosanna!' after him. It seems he can manipulate the minds of children too, given the opportunity."

"This is not true."

The words were spoken, clearly and loudly, by the councillor at Joseph's side; a man in his early forties who did not try to hide the indignation in his voice.

Zibeon turned to stare at the speaker with quick hostility.

The man went on, "If Zibeon wants to speak of matters like manipulation of the mind, then let him talk about the special privileges he contrived to sell this month for so-called 'voluntary contributions' to the Treasury! Moneys it is known he needed to support his aged father!"

Caiaphas turned angrily. "I will not have accusations of that kind voiced at a time like this, Nicodemus! You're well aware that you have a proper channel for such allegations."

Joseph was on his feet before he knew it, his anger burning at the lot of them.

"What Nicodemus says is true, though! You know as

51

well as I do that those proper channels you speak about are clogged with written protests that are never answered! And now's as good a time as any to remind you of it. If any member of the great Sanhedrin has a particle of conscience left to him these days, he has to stifle it. He has to put it on a shelf to wait a more convenient season. He has to go on waiting until a handful of the Council have decided if there's aught in such a protest that might offend the Romans—or while the bulk of you below the Council here debate how best to twist the matter to your own profit, to your purses, or to your latest shallow-brained interpretation of the Law! I hold no brief for this man Jesus. For all I know he may be just as dangerous as most of you believe. But his appeal to the people lies in part in our excesses. We must clean our own house—that will take away any threat he poses. And I do know that Nicodemus merits a fair hearing—on anything he may choose to say!"

There was a loud general outcry from the assembly, and Zibeon's own tongue flamed up at what he said. "Joseph of Arimathea's been spoiling for a fight since listening to that latoot little pack of lies spread by some troublemaker here a day or two ago. Your nephew, my lord Caiaphas, has not yet learned to separate fable from fact. He swallows all he hears so greedily that now he thinks he has good cause to fight the whole Sanhedrin!"

Caiaphas was white with anger. "Silence, Zibeon! You

will be silent too, Joseph. And Nicodemus ... if you've aught to say on the subject under discussion we will listen to you."

Nicodemus was still resolutely on his feet, and he seemed perfectly composed.

"I was a witness of these happenings too," he said. "I came through Solomon's Porch as Jesus reached it. And I assure you that the anger he had shown against the moneychangers had altogether vanished by the time he turned to the women and children who had followed him with their menfolk. I don't believe he had the slightest wish to preach revolt to any of those children. They seemed to follow him as if they wanted to. I saw him take the hand of the small boy ... the child of that woman Rhoda you know about...."

"Rhoda?" Caiaphas repeated the name as a quick question, but even as he said it, there came into his eyes some shadow of unpleasant recognition.

"The woman Rhoda, from the Street of Weavers," Nicodemus explained. "The one who was stoned for adultery last month."

The ragged whisper was proof enough they knew of what he spoke. But the whisper came and went, and when Nicodemus dropped his voice a little, the hall had grown so still that every man could hear what he said next.

"They say the little fellow watched it happen—though heaven knows why his kinsfolk failed to keep him from such a spectacle. He tried to stop them casting stones at her, but he must have barely come up to their knees. How could a child like that begin to understand? Finally they carried him away from it all, kicking and screaming. Since then I've heard that he's run away from all men."

Nicodemus paused there, watching, defiantly surveying Caiaphas' face for a moment before continuing.

"He didn't have the slightest fear of running to this Nazarene. I saw the child come out from somewhere in the crowd behind him, and it almost seemed as if Jesus must have known that he was coming. He turned around, stooped and smiled, then held his arms open to the child. And the two of them went off together hand in hand along the colonnade."

"And that was where," cried Zibeon, across the heads of all the men around him, "the multitude began to shout again, just as they'd shouted at the Sheep Gate—'Blessed be the King that cometh in the name of the Lord!'"

The High Priest had risen to silence Zibeon again, but the murmuring of the crowd in front of him now made him hesitate. Long skilled in the use of mood and moment, Caiaphas made the most of it. He stepped to the edge of the platform, conscious of their faith that as High Priest of Israel, Aaron's own gift of prophecy had descended through the generations upon him.

"Make no mistake, there's nothing but disaster for us if we fail to put an end to what this man is doing. Nor is the

Sanhedrin blameless for what's going on. When this Nazarene was in Galilee his doings seemed to us of little consequence. . . ."

One of the Pharisees called out, "Is blasphemy of little consequence? Or breaking the Sabbath? Or defying the Law? Or overriding the Tradition. . . ?"

"It's far more urgent, Jonah, that we've let these heresies of his grow fast enough to win the people! While we've been talking calmly of him here among ourselves, while we've been deluding ourselves that naught of any great importance ever came from Galilee, this wily Galilean has been moving with the cunning of Beelzebub. He's been astute enough to wait until the multitudes are pouring into town to celebrate the holiday. He's waited for the hundreds of thousands to assemble here—from north, south, east and west! He knows that whatever he can do here now will be noised about in Tyre and Sidon and Athens and in Rome. And Rome, let me remind you all, is also in Jerusalem."

An aged voice was bold enough to fling a taunt towards the platform. "Then heaven be praised that so many of your fellow Sadducees have found such excellent means of stopping the ears of Rome at times like this!"

There was a mutter of bitter laughter once again. It grew so threatening that Malachi from his place at the High Priest's side broke in once more to save the situation. "If we have any wish to keep alive what's left of our authority, then let's give Caiaphas the deference expected of us. I beg silence for him."

Caiaphas gave a nod of quick relief and took a step back from the edge of the platform. It emphasized what Malachi had said, for it set ringing the row of miniature bells on the hem of his robe again; a clear reminder of High Priestly power.

He leaned toward the watching faces and said emphatically, "What we decide to do about this Nazarene must be done before the Passover is eaten. What have you all to say about it?"

Caiaphas sat in his seat again, and there was a rush of talk beneath him.

"Why not have him seized as a disturber of the peace?" called one, "and have him held until the feast is over."

The Suffragan, who had been listening watchfully, ventured a cautious, "That would still leave the matter to be dealt with afterwards, and it would give him extra time to win more people."

"How would you set about arresting him?" asked another. "You'd have to seize the multitude itself. They would defend him with their lives, I think."

Zibeon threw in his own suggestion. "Then why not have him seized by night?"

A murmur of approval greeted the idea. But Nicodemus rose to protest.

"There is no single accusation, my lord Caiaphas, on which there's any evidence against this man save contradictory gossip and opinion."

The others looked at Nicodemus with impatience, but Malachi, a stickler for the truth, supported him. "What Nicodemus says is at any rate open to discussion. Here in this hall we represent the Law, and let us not forget it." He stared at them as if to emphasize his words, then dropped his voice a little. "If we ourselves fail to follow the Law, how can we expect to find obedience in others?"

Caiaphas was quick to take his cue. "If we make a false step now," he said, "this Nazarene may start not just another burst of civil strife, but the final one. And what could Pilate do but intervene? Let's not delude ourselves! With things in Israel as they are today, there can't be such a thing as a contained revolt. It would sweep through the land like wildfire, all the way from Galilee to Egypt. It would engulf the nation. And that, need I add, would mean an end to the Sanhedrin."

"What do you propose we do about it?"

Caiaphas responded carefully. "I suggest that a delegation from this body, a handful of shrewd men picked for their skill in the Law, go out and talk to this man Jesus in the Temple. As soon as they have reached a common strategy, this delegation will secure unquestionable evidence, the kind of evidence we can proceed on. It must be clear enough for the crowd to realize that in opposing us they would oppose the Law itself—and thus bring on their own undoing."

"Let us agree to this," called out a voice.

"But let's make sure we know just where we stand!" cried another. "He is a cunning adversary, this Galilean, as many of us know already. He makes himself so plausible and seems so full of knowledge, even though he's scarcely over thirty."

Caiaphas had an answer for that warning also.

"Then we will match him as to years and better him in argument. I recommend that we send Zibeon here, with his friend Ephraim; the two work well together. And also Sharmah. And Joseph of Arimathea."

The High Priest paused there, and when he spoke again a tinge of cynicism was in his voice. "Joseph has expert knowledge of the Law," he said. "And with his burning wish to cleanse us of corruption, he might recognize more readily the illegalities in others. Perhaps in such a frame of mind he'll help to rid us of this troublemaker."

The High Priest looked directly into Joseph's face, and yet continued to address the whole assembly. "I think there may be other pressing reasons why our friend from Arimathea might want to prove his value to the Council at a time like this."

Joseph returned the gaze of Caiaphas steadfastly, sharply conscious of the matter in the High Priest's mind.

MAN BEFORE THE MORNING

In the moment that the two men stared at one another, Joseph saw beyond the glint of challenge in the other's face. He remembered Drusilla's suspicion that Caiaphas might try to test him in some way. He remembered too her plea that he should not be a thorn in the Sanhedrin's side, but up and leading them.

But Joseph knew that he could not bind himself even for Drusilla's sake to say just what was expected of him. He didn't know any longer what was right to say or ask. But he knew he could not be the hypocrite that some of them would have him be! He would judge for himself and then tell the truth.

Yet he recalled Sosthenes' words: "Let's not risk shortening such a time as you have left with her, Joseph, by any cause for grieving." And he felt guilty. He could not balance his principles and his love.

Joseph grew conscious that the other men who had been named were giving their agreement.

Zibeon was all too eager. So was the colorless Ephraim, sitting there beside him. And Sharmah also gave assent.

"And you, Joseph?"

Joseph looked earnestly at Caiaphas and then at Malachi, reading the extra burden of anxiety on his foster-father's face.

"I'll do as the Sanhedrin wishes about it," he said quietly. And turned to face another kind of apprehension, this time a much more baffling look, on the face of

MAN BEFORE THE MORNING

Nicodemus, sitting there beside him. But he paid him no mind; his thoughts were on another matter. One he dreaded. It was a task he knew he must do—as a test and proof of his love. So reluctantly but with haste he left the assembly to go while he yet had time to that forbidding quarter of the city. There he would buy for himself and for his beloved wife a tomb.

CHAPTER
3

It had been agreed that the four of them—Joseph, Sharmah, Zibeon and Ephraim—should meet outside the main door of the Chamber of Hewn Stone as soon as Ephraim had performed one of his daily duties of the week, that of renewing the incense for the second service.

Joseph had gone quickly about his dreaded business and completed it swiftly and satisfactorily. He purchased a newly made sepulchre. And endeavored to put the incident entirely from his mind.

But Zibeon and Ephraim had not arrived at the prearranged place at the expected time. And Joseph waited there with the aging Sharmah, aching to go off into the center court of the Temple and confront this Jesus

MAN BEFORE THE MORNING

without the help of Zibeon and that unctuous friend of his. After his unhappy duties regarding the tomb, he felt nervous, depressed and almost eager to face a fight with the Nazarene and his band.

Until the altar ceremony was over, however, he could not move, and he was glad that the singing of the prescribed prayer was almost finished.

The sea of silent faces around him served only to sharpen the restless waiting. The glint and glitter of the afternoon sun threw everything into such bold relief that it appeared to give an extra urgency to their task.

The marble of the walls to his left and the splendor of the colonnade to his right, the gold of the Gate Beautiful from which the steps led down into the Court of the Women, the billowing wreaths of sepia smoke from the incense on the altar (its perfume, this afternoon, strong enough to smother even the sickening reek of burning flesh, still all but shuddering from the sacrificial knife)—all these stood out today with extra clarity.

With their backs to the Holy Place and their silver trumpets ready at their lips, the usual row of priests stood on each side of the steps in front of him. Between them the choir of the Levites and the accompanying musicians with their harps and lutes stood facing the Holy Place, singing the last few stanzas of the psalm selected for the day:

MAN BEFORE THE MORNING

Walk about Zion, and go round about her.
Tell the towers thereof.

Mark ye well her bulwarks,
Consider her palaces;
That ye may tell it to the generation following.

For this God is our God, for ever and ever;
He will be our guide even unto death.

That was the end of it. As the musicians lowered their harps and the waiting priests sounded three blasts upon their trumpets, the people bowed in worship. Then the service was over.

Now the long succession of private sacrifices, the purifications, the special offerings for special purposes would resume. Already, in fact, the space was fast returning to its bustle of renewed activity. And among the busy people moving in all directions, Joseph at last saw Zibeon and Ephraim coming toward him.

There was little pleasure in the discovery for it was an unholy kind of partnership those two had. The weaker Ephraim not only agreed with most things that the superior Zibeon said, but even tended to imitate his friend's considerable repertoire of gestures.

With barely a pause for greeting, Zibeon said, "We have been talking about the quickest way of getting this

Nazarene to stop airing generalities and get down to basic facts—facts about himself, of course."

Sharmah cleared his throat and began to speak. Perhaps it was the perpetual ache in his back that made him sound somewhat petulant. "If the two of you'd been here when you should have been we could have gone over our plan together before all this movement and confusion started up again. There's nothing worse than being half prepared about these things."

With but a glance at Sharmah, Joseph turned to Zibeon, "Did you come to any conclusion?"

It was Ephraim who gave the short, sly nod of affirmation. He spoke for his friend as if he had been nudged to do so. "Zibeon has thought of a little device to put this Jesus just where we want him: in open opposition to the Romans."

"And what is that?" asked Joseph.

Zibeon himself said smoothly, "Why don't you wait and see? Discussing it here might waste a lot of time. The man's out there already. And that's another reason that we're late. We wanted to make sure of him."

"He's in Solomon's Porch," confirmed Ephraim. "With quite a crowd around him."

"Enough of one," said Zibeon, "so that we should move quickly before they get too many to handle."

"If you had years to match your haste, Zibeon," protested

Sharmah testily, "you might have learned that sometimes the easiest way to handle a crowd is to be part of it."

Joseph nodded. "The fact that we're together doesn't mean we have to look like a delegation. Not one of the four of us—not even you, Zibeon—is well enough known among those people to be spotted immediately. Let's mingle with them and listen to him for a while."

But Sharmah was shaking his head. "What I meant," he said, "was something different." But like the others, he was already falling more or less into step as they went through the gate and down into the courtyard beyond.

"What I meant," he repeated, "was that since the crowd flatters him—and he seems to thrive on it—let's not be above a little flattery too. Praise, you know, can open the ears of even the stubbornest men and wag their tongues to useful purpose."

Joseph looked sideways at the older man, feeling a wave of irritation at Sharmah's brazen confidence. But at least they stayed together as they strode along. And they were out now in the broad and crowded area of the Court of the Gentiles.

Zibeon threw at Joseph a smile without warmth. "Your Uncle Caiaphas," he said, "seemed to suggest that you were even more eager to distinguish yourself than usual, Joseph. You must be glad of the chance."

Ephraim, riding on the crest of his friend's sarcasm,

ventured a grunt of laughter. "Caiaphas made us curious, Joseph, about why you had a special need just now to show your skill at squeezing evidence out of a man. Perhaps there is some private reason. We mustn't intrude."

Joseph made no comment. He felt the color rising to his cheeks and clenched his fists. The smoothness of his walk began to take on the sharpness of a march. He compelled himself to think of nothing but the scene in front of him.

There was the usual crowd of pilgrims. There was the same old flurry of multi-colored movement in the sun, of shifting robes in red and purple—saffron, brown and blue—of ponderous rabbis in impressive black and hurrying priests in white. There was nothing that met his eyes to indicate the possibility of any civil strife or insurrection. There was no sign of tension in the crowd—only in him.

Over them all was the earthy chatter of country accents, ways of speech that hailed from every corner of the compass. Interlaced through this mesh of sound was the bleating of bewildered sheep and the cooing of doves.

At last he saw a separate crowd over in the double colonnade of the porch of Solomon, a crowd that seemed to be growing thicker about the edges, an irregular oval of men and women and a few children too gathered around some focal point beside one of the pillars.

MAN BEFORE THE MORNING

A curious anxiety grew in Joseph as they drew closer. For a few more moments the general sounds in the Temple courts prevented him from hearing what the man was saying, but this fact enabled him to concentrate the more on what he saw.

He had seen this Nazarene once before. That had been upon the slopes of Olivet in the far distance. Today as he came closer he saw that Jesus did not look at all like a disturber of the peace. It was in fact hard to believe that this man had held a scourge so recently and used it, according to report, with such effect.

Today the man was standing there, his arms outstretched a little to the crowds, his hands extended, welcoming and giving.

He seemed a tall, commanding figure as he stood against the pillar. He wore a plain white mantle with a simple traveling cloak thrown over his shoulder. He had the healthy tan of a young man who lived in sun and rain, and there was a brightness about his eyes that was quite manifest even from the edge of the crowd.

The four from the Sanhedrin came into the outer ring of the crowd at last, and gradually edged themselves among the others until they could see and hear distinctly.

The voice of Jesus was clear and vigorous, full of the fresh-air cadences of Galilee. It was the voice of a countryman, with the echo of the hills in it. And though he spoke without elaboration, there was a simple and uncultivated eloquence about him that held his audience motionless.

Now and then he paused to look at the ring of faces in front of him to see how much they understood of what he said, and sometimes he stopped to answer their questions.

Around him were the few disciples of his own particular choosing, the men who now followed him wherever he went. But the crowd about him also seemed to be made up of faithful followers for the most part.

Not all the watching faces though were clearly friendly. Joseph recognized, standing not far from him, some of the Pharisees who were not of the Sanhedrin, men who had been agitating from the outside for the seizure of this man. They were scattered in the crowd, watching in disapproval. Others also looked like unbelievers. They had been drawn by their curiosity no doubt to listen to the man of whom they had already heard such wild, improbable tales.

"I am the light of the world," he was saying. "No follower of mine shall wander in the dark. He shall have the light of life!"

One of the Pharisees near Joseph in the crowd appeared to resent this promise. "You are a witness in your own cause," he shouted. "Your testimony is not valid."

Jesus replied, "My testimony is valid, even though I do

bear witness of myself: because I know where I come from and where I am going. You do not know either where I come from or where I am going. You judge by worldly standards. I pass judgment on no man, but if I do judge, my judgment is valid, because it is not I alone who judge, but I and He who sent me. In your own law, it is written that the testimony of two witnesses is valid. Here I am, a witness in my own cause, and my other witness is the Father who sent me."

Another of the listening men called out "Where is your father?"

Jesus looked steadfastly across at him. "You know not me nor my Father," he replied. "If you knew me, you would know my Father also."

A woman next to Joseph whispered to her neighbor, "This must be the expected prophet! Who else could speak with such authority?"

The word "authority" seemed to the listening Sharmah as if it were the cue for which he had been waiting.

He called to Jesus, and the Nazarene turned to look at him.

"By what authority," asked Sharmah, "are you acting like this? Who gave you authority to act in this way?"

"And this time," called another, hostile voice, "tell us clearly, Galilean! This is a question that concerns a lot of us."

Jesus kept his eyes on the first speaker. "I have a question that concerns you too," he said quietly. "Tell me, was the baptism of John from God or from men?"

The question sent a wave of curiosity around the crowd. It was vociferous enough for Sharmah to say, almost as much to himself as to Joseph, "If we say 'from God' he will say 'Why did you not believe him?' And, if we say 'from men' the people will stone us, for they are convinced that John was a prophet."

Joseph glanced at the Nazarene with quickened interest.

Aloud, Sharmah said weakly, and with the irritation of defeat, "I cannot tell."

The calm eyes of the Nazarene regarded him a moment longer. "Neither will I tell you by what authority I act," he said.

Zibeon's lips curled into a slow, ingratiating smile. With a slight tilting of the head he said, "Master, you are an honest man, we know. You teach in all honesty the way of life that God requires, truckling to no man, whoever he may be. Give us your ruling on this, then: are we or are we not permitted to pay taxes to the Roman Emperor?" He paused a moment, then added smoothly, "Shall we pay or not?"

Joseph glanced quickly from one to the other, finding himself, despite the reason for his presence here, hoping the Nazarene would see beyond the wretched subterfuge.

MAN BEFORE THE MORNING

Jesus looked at Zibeon and Ephraim, and upon the faces of the other Pharisees who had been heckling him. And the scorn on his face showed how clearly he had read their purpose. "You hypocrites!" he said. "Why do you lay a trap for me like this? Show me the money in which the tax is paid."

Without losing for a moment his obsequious smile, Zibeon nodded to Ephraim, and Ephraim slipped his hand into the bag at his waist, taking from it a silver piece which he handed over as requested.

"Whose head is this, and whose inscription?" Jesus asked.

"Caesar's," they answered quickly.

"Then pay Caesar what is due to Caesar," Jesus answered simply, "and pay God what is due to God."

Ephraim pocketed the silver piece amid a ripple of laughter from those in the crowd who were bold enough to let the Pharisees know how they felt about his obvious embarrassment.

Beneath the flutter of ridicule Sharmah muttered an aside to Joseph—"Didn't I warn them? This is what comes of leaping into a situation half prepared!"

But Joseph's eyes had now been caught by a woman standing across from him on the other inner edge of the crowd. He did not know her; as far as he could tell he had never before set eyes on her. But he was surprised to see a look of obvious pity for him on her face.

MAN BEFORE THE MORNING

He was not used to pity. He did not welcome it. Yet for a fleeting moment her penetrating sympathy was unmistakable.

Noting his eyes upon her the woman turned her gaze away to Jesus. And as she did so her expressive face, glimpsed in the blue-brown shadow of her veil, took on a look of gratitude that made Joseph wonder.

She obviously had not been one of those who laughed at the discomfiture of Zibeon and Ephraim. She seemed in fact quite detached from the passions of the crowd, as if she had found in the presence of the Nazarene something that held her undisturbed and above such things. Her face was not especially beautiful, he thought, yet something linked to this same scene had given her a composure he had seldom seen in a woman.

She made a little gesture with her hands—a mere touch of the pin brooch on her shoulder—and the gesture reminded him of Drusilla. He remembered some of the things she had spoken only yesterday, aware of neither her own peril nor his confusion.

"When I'm strong enough to go back into Jerusalem with you," she had said, "I want to watch you striding there beside me, and I want to hear them whispering to one another, as we go by, 'That's Joseph, you know, Joseph of Arimathea. The one who's turning the tide....'"

He shook his head in sudden self-disgust, knowing that far from turning the tide, he had merely choosen to drift with it. He had agreed in the Sanhedrin that if there were any truth in the idea that Jesus was a grave threat to the people, he would probe that threat and bring it out into the open where it could be dealt with legally.

Yet at the moment he was not even listening to the man! He was thinking instead about Drusilla. After a little while, though, it seemed as if Jesus' calm, clear voice began to pull him back into its message once again.

"Now about the resurrection of the dead," said Jesus. "Have you not read in the book of Moses, in the story of the burning bush, how God spoke to him and said 'I am the God of Abraham, the God of Isaac, and the God of Jacob?' God is not a God of the dead but of the living!"

Joseph's attention focused on those four short words—"the book of Moses." If there were talk about the book of Moses, then here was solid ground, more worthy ground, on which to search for any public danger in the man. And at the heart of the Law of Moses were the Ten Commandments.

Perhaps if it were possible to probe the attitude of Jesus to the Ten Commandments there might appear some clue, some line of evidence....

Joseph did not stop to follow his train of thought any further. He simply faced the speaker.

"Which commandment," he asked boldly, "is first of all?"

Jesus turned to look at him.

MAN BEFORE THE MORNING

It was the first time that their eyes had met. Yet Joseph knew as he looked that despite the errand that had brought him here he looked into the face of a friend. There was a curious warmth of recognition here. It was as if for a moment the clear brown eyes were saying, "So you are Joseph. I'm going to need you."

Aloud the Nazarene answered Joseph's spoken question.

"The first," he said, "is 'Hear, O Israel, the Lord your God is the only Lord. Love the Lord your God with all your heart, with all your soul, with all your mind, and with all your strength.' And the second is this: 'Love your neighbor as yourself.' There is no other commandment greater than these."

For a moment Joseph pondered the familiar words, and not just the words but the way in which Jesus said them. There was no flouting of the Law of Moses in that voice, none of the heresy that rumor said he should expect. There was instead a love of the Commandments. There was a reverence for them, the same clear recognition of their power and beauty that Joseph himself still glimpsed at times beneath the web the Pharisees had spread across them.

For a moment the whole crowd, including Sharmah, Zibeon, and Ephraim, ceased to exist for him, so that he was left alone there in the Temple facing the man he had been sent to condemn.

He heard himself responding, "Well said, Master! You're

right in saying God is one, and beside him there is no other. And to love him with all your heart, all your understanding and all your strength, and to love your neighbor as yourself—that is far more than any burnt offerings or sacrifices!"

There was a moment's pause. Then Jesus smiled at last—a joyful smile. And he looked into the face of Joseph and said quietly, "You are not far from the Kingdom of God!"

Then Jesus turned to his disciples again, while Joseph just stood there staring at him.

A frightening question started to assert itself in him. What if they're right, he asked himself? *What if they're right*, these crowds that follow him with all their sick and maimed? And a deeper, far more shattering doubt arose: What if this man in his white mantle and his simple traveling cloak were the Messiah whom Israel had been awaiting? What if he *is* the answer to the prophecies?"

The years of Sadducean unbringing, the rigid attitudes that had surrounded him since he had come as a mere child into the house of Malachi—all these and other prejudices rose in violent opposition to the thought. And all the warnings that foretold the coming of false prophets, the nature of the sinners with whom this man consorted, his so-called casting out of devils with the aid of Beelzebub, these things had drummed into Joseph a fierce, concerted NO.

But his heart told him otherwise.

MAN BEFORE THE MORNING

He had to remind himself that he was here at the behest of the Sanhedrin. He tried to remember that whatever he might say or do here that would disgrace his foster-father could cause Drusilla unneeded worry.

But once again that voice was ringing in his ears. "The Father loves me because I lay down my life to receive it back again. No one has robbed me of it; I am laying it down of my own free will. I have the right to lay it down, and I have the right to receive it back again; this charge I have received from my Father."

A sallow-faced man near Joseph shouted out, "He is possessed! Can't you tell the man is raving?"

"Why," asked another, "do we go on standing here, listening to this nonsense?"

Another angry voice across the ring of faces took up the threat. "He is indeed possessed of a devil!" A woman's treble tried to rebuke the charge. "No one possessed of a devil could speak as he does! Could a devil open blind men's eyes?"

"Listen to her!" called out one of the Pharisees. "There is proof of how he works on them!"

"Be careful how you speak of him, Pharisee!" warned another. "Remember well of whom you speak!"

"He is the Messiah!" cried an old man. And a young woman, holding close to her breast an infant, asked aloud, "Doesn't the Scripture say that the Messiah is to be of the family of David—from David's village of Bethlehem?"

76

MAN BEFORE THE MORNING

But Jesus stood there calmly, untouched by the contention that blazed about him.

"For a little longer," he was saying, "I shall be with you: then I am going away to him who sent me. You will look for me, but you will not find me. Where I am going you cannot come."

"Perhaps he will kill himself," Ephraim murmured. "Is that what he means?"

Sharmah who had been watching silently so long called out to Jesus quite distinctly then, "Who are you?"

"When you have lifted up the Son of Man," Jesus replied, "you will know that I am what I am. I do nothing on my own authority, but in all that I say I have been taught of my Father. He who sent me is present with me, and has not left me alone; for I always do what is acceptable to him."

"And if God should be his Father," cried a woman, looking directly at Sharmah, "then all of us who try to do the will of God must be his disciples too!"

The thought appeared to sharpen the irritation of the Pharisees. But now, Joseph noted, the other three of the Sanhedrin delegation remained as silent as he did himself.

Jesus explained, "If you dwell within the revelation I have brought, you are indeed my disciples; you shall know the truth, and the truth shall make you free."

"What do you mean by that?" called one of the hecklers. "We are Abraham's descendants: we have never been in slavery to any man!"

"Why do you not understand my language?" asked the Nazarene. "It is because my revelation is beyond your grasp. Your father is the devil, and you choose to carry out your father's desires. He was a murderer from the beginning, and is not rooted in the truth; there is no truth in him. When he tells a lie he is speaking his own language, for he is a liar and the father of lies. But I speak the truth, and therefore you do not believe me."

Jesus let his gaze pass over the faces of those who had been questioning him.

"Which of you convicts me of sin?" he asked.

Only the general increasing murmur of the crowd served as his answer.

"If what I say is true, why do you not believe me? He who has God for his father listens to the word of God. You are not God's children; that is why you do not listen."

One of the Pharisees who stood quite close to him cried scornfully, and as much to the crowd as to Jesus, "Aren't we right in saying you're a Samaritan? And that you are possessed?"

"I am not possessed," said Jesus; "the truth is that I am honoring my Father, but you dishonor me. In very truth I tell you if anyone obeys my teaching, he shall never know what it is to die."

"Listen to him!" cried an old man near Joseph. And the voices of those who were against him rose on every side. Another shouted, "Abraham is dead; the prophets are dead; and yet you say 'If anyone obeys my teaching he shall not know what it is to die!' "

"Your father Abraham rejoiced to see my day," said Jesus. "He saw it and was glad!"

The words brought hollow laughter. "You're not yet fifty years old!" they mocked him. "How can you have seen Abraham?"

"In very truth," said Jesus, "I tell you, before Abraham was, I am."

"Possessed!" they shouted. "Did we not tell you he was possessed? Listen to a man who has a devil!"

Jesus looked at them with deep compassion. And at length he raised his eyes and gestured toward the Temple courts and the city beyond.

"O Jerusalem, Jerusalem!" he said, ". . . the city that murders the prophets and stones the messengers sent to her! How often have I longed to gather your children, as a hen gathers her brood under her wings, but you would not let me. Look, look! There is your Temple—forsaken by God!"

Joseph looked sharply at the familiar outlines of the Temple. "Forsaken by God," this Galilean said. And the terrifying realization came to him that the accusation could be true.

The words were a charge against the Pharisees, whose concentration on the administration of the Law was hiding the love that used to shine behind the Law. The words were in fact an accusation against all the hatreds of this day and age—the blinding hate between the Pharisees and the Sadducees, the hate that seethed around the Romans, Samaritans and Herodians, the all-consuming overwhelming hate against the Gentiles.

There was an outburst of noisy anger from the crowd.

"Let's show this man he cannot stand there, in the Temple itself, uttering these blasphemies!" yelled a voice.

Beneath the growing hubbub Sharmah said, "There seem to be more people against him now than there are for him. If that's the case, why should we fear his followers so much that we daren't lay a finger on him?"

Joseph shook his head. "Wait!" he warned. "These you see here are but a handful from a multitude that covers all the land. But even these I think would rush to aid him if the Temple police were ordered out to seize him."

"Are you all blind?" cried one of the Nazarene's disciples. "Can you not see he is no lunatic?"

"Ask them, those Pharisees," called another voice, "if they're not only blind but deaf as well! No man ever spoke as does this man!"

"Or worked such wonders!" cried the thin voice of a woman.

"Stone him!" screamed one of the troublemakers.

"Drag him from the Temple! Stone him!" yelled another. And instantly a din of other hostile voices in the crowd took up the threat.

MAN BEFORE THE MORNING

His followers started closing round him. There was a quickening of movement in the crowd. Then suddenly, it seemed to Joseph as he watched, there was no sign of Jesus there at all. Nor did his followers seem startled by the fact.

One of them cried out as if in explanation, "He said his time had not yet come."

"And you who seek his life shall not discover him," called out another.

Wondering, bewildered, yet certain somehow that the man they followed was quite safe, his followers began to scatter.

Joseph saw Sharmah leave also—silently and with frustration on his sallow face. As for Zibeon and his friend Ephraim he could not see them now.

He stood there motionless, a storm of doubt and helplessness inside him.

Then it was he noticed the woman again. Her ordinary face still held that extraordinary beauty. And she was looking at him once again.

Unreasonably something about her calmness angered him. No man or woman had the right to be so bathed in such serenity at such a time. Impelled by his impatience he went over to her.

"Woman," he said, "I've watched you watching him. How can you be so peaceful at a time like this?"

She did not directly answer the question. But after a

moment's pause she said simply, "I have been watching you also, sir. I think you are much troubled."

"I did not speak of any trouble," he said shortly.

"There was no need to speak of it," she said, looking at him without resentment. And then, "He who was talking here just now could help you."

"I want nothing to do with him."

"I wonder if you mean that, sir."

"What makes you sound so sure that he could help?"

She smiled at him, a kindly smile, more full of understanding than of pity.

"You'd find the best of answers to that question," she said, "in the house my husband and I are staying in until the feast is over. It is my sister's house. I wonder if you'd let me ... show you this answer."

He looked at her. She was quite obviously a stranger in Jerusalem, and clearly a countrywoman. She may have guessed from his clothes and his manner of speech that he was a Sadducee. But there was something warm and curiously urgent in her invitation.

"My sister's house is very close, sir—just over the Kidron on the road to Bethany." After a moment she added "I think it would be good if you could come."

He hesitated. He should be on his way back to report to Caiaphas, no matter how inept and foolish his report might be. And more importantly he should be going home again to Drusilla, and his heart was already aching at the questions she would ask him.

Somehow or other though the situation seemed to be taking care of itself.

"It's kind of you," he heard himself saying to the woman. "I will come with you, though I cannot stay very long."

"My name is Miriam," she said, turning to lead the way. And then as if she felt a need to add to this, "My husband's name is Jairus. We are from Bethsaida."

CHAPTER
4

Regardless of the fact that by now the Sanhedrin would be expecting him and Caiaphas would be awaiting a report of what had happened, Joseph was glad at last to cross the bridge over the Kidron. For though it was only a short bridge it seemed, once they began to climb the winding road up the slopes of Olivet on the other side, to have separated them at last from all the tumult and turmoil, all the sights and sounds of the vast Temple behind them. It even seemed to have separated them from Jerusalem itself, though with the wind in the west like this the throb and murmur of those multitudes still sounded in his ears like the hum of some agitated beehive.

Yet in the company of this woman who walked beside

him there was happiness and peace. She did not seem to grow fatigued by the rapid pace they were making; in fact she moved gracefully and smoothly, her simple brown and saffron robe floating quite lightly with her as she walked. Even the startling question she asked him did not rob the moment of its peace.

"I think, sir, you are Joseph, aren't you? Joseph of Arimathea, of the Council of the Sanhedrin?"

He looked at her closely, wondering if she had known this all along.

"When I mentioned my husband's name, sir, I don't think you remembered it. Jairus is an Elder in the little synagogue in Bethsaida. When you came to Galilee to check the scrolls my husband was the one who met you."

"I'm sorry I don't remember him. I visited so many synagogues."

After a little pause she said, "It may not be too wise for me to bring a Scribe of the Sanhedrin to my sister's house. But while I watched you, sir, as you stood there with the others you looked so troubled that I wanted you to know a wondrous thing that I know about Jesus."

"Why did you think then that it might be better for me not to come with you?"

"We are his followers," she said simply.

"Your husband too?" The question echoed his surprise.

She gave him a look of quick concern as she walked beside him.

MAN BEFORE THE MORNING

"Up in Bethsaida," she said, "we don't know what you've heard about him in Jerusalem, but I believe that if you could see some of the good he's done in Galilee you might be able to think of him as Jairus does. People in the synagogue are blessed to have him read the Law to them."

"What if he breaks the Law?"

She walked beside him silently a moment, looking straight ahead. It was almost as if she listened for an answer.

"He says he didn't come among us to destroy the Law, sir, but to fulfill it. I believe the Prophets foretold that he would come."

From the long grasses by the roadside a lapwing rose, the sun aglitter on his feathers as he soared and trilled his song across the broom and myrtle into the shadow of a juniper tree. And from over the green brow of the hill they could now hear the faint cool trickle of running water. It was one of the spring-filled brooks that turned toward the Kidron.

In obvious skepticism Joseph asked pointedly, "Do you agree then with these fantastic claims made by some people that he is the Messiah?"

She smiled at that. It was an assured, untroubled smile. "There's one in my family, sir, who might answer that question without speaking any words."

"Jairus?"

She shook her head. "No, sir. My husband won't be

there just now; he's gone with Simeon, my brother-in-law, to make some more arrangements for the Passover. My sister Naomi is at home, though, and her three children. But the one I speak of is my own child, and she's at home here with them too. Her name's Rebecca."

"What makes you think a girl could convince me—or others?"

They turned away now from the road along a path that led past one of the small olive groves toward the south and the village of Bethphage. Close in front of them there was a cluster of houses along the hillside.

"Because Rebecca herself is the answer, sir. One of so many answers you could find in Galilee."

"You speak in mysteries," he said.

She halted on the path beside him, not because she was fatigued but in order to explain without distraction. He too stopped and listened with curiosity as they talked, glad to feel on his face the breath of the breeze that rose in the hills. It was enough of a breeze to stir the folds of her simple robe. And he wondered at himself—allowing himself to be led so easily in such curious circumstances by a woman, one he didn't even know.

"Rebecca died," she said quietly.

He turned to look at her sharply. It was obviously not a part of any riddle that she spoke. She did not seem the type of woman to be given to delusions. And there was something new in her eyes as she looked at him now. It was a kind of remembered wonder.

88

MAN BEFORE THE MORNING

He said, "I thought you told me she was waiting for you here in your sister's house."

"She is, sir. She's playing with the other children, I expect."

"Then what...?" He did not finish the question; a sudden hush came upon him, as if he stood upon the threshold of some miracle.

"It was so short a time ago," she said. "Rebecca had been ill for many days with a high fever. We do not have a very experienced physician in Bethsaida, but he did his best for us. There came a morning when he told us that he couldn't save her."

"I *know* how hard that must have been for you."

"Jairus got so frightened that he could do naught but sit there, his hands upon Rebecca's hand, muttering some words I couldn't understand. But I remembered what I'd heard of Jesus and of the healing works they said he'd done in Galilee. My neighbor Sara told me that he'd just gotten back from the country of the Gadarenes. So I begged Jairus there and then to run down to the market-place in search of him."

"And did he go?"

"He would have gone on any journey that might have helped Rebecca."

"Did he find him?"

She nodded. "He found him in the middle of a crowd. And Jairus never had so terrible a testing time, for even while he begged Jesus to come home to us some other

woman sought his help. Jairus had to wait there. But he
told me afterwards that even while he stood there shaking with anxiety he slowly grew aware that Jesus could
and would help. And even when I sent our servant Silas
down to tell my husband that Rebecca had stopped
breathing, that it was too late, my husband said he still
had faith. Jesus told him not to fear and came home with
him at last.

"There was such noisy weeping and lamenting around
our house by that time that Jesus had to tell them to be
quiet. And he brought three of his close disciples into the
house," she paused a moment, her eyes lost in the
memory.

"And then?" Joseph asked.

"Then he came gently to Rebecca's bed and looked at
her. He didn't seem to be distressed about her. He lifted
up her hand and raised his eyes, seeing some wonder that
set his face aglow. And then he said, "Get up, my child!"
And as he held her hand, I saw her eyelids tremble and
presently she got up and smiled."

Rebecca's mother stopped there; she looked at Joseph
with such peace of heart. He too was moved and couldn't
think of anything else to ask her.

"Back in the Temple, sir," she continued, "you looked so
worried that I wanted you to meet Rebecca for yourself,
for even though she's just a child, she is a witness. Now
that we're here, I'm going to call the other children back

inside the house, so you can stay here in the courtyard and talk with her."

The laughter of the children already reached them as they walked into the open courtyard of a house that was a little bigger than the others, though still a modest place, tucked in a grove of oaks and olive trees.

Naomi, Miriam's sister (probably, Joseph thought, somewhat older) came out as they reached the house and Miriam introduced her.

Three children laughed excitedly beneath a carob tree, two girls and a small boy. They must have been Naomi's children, for when at the bidding of Miriam Naomi called to them to go inside the house for a while, all three of them rather reluctantly obeyed her. The little boy, however, kept throwing eager, backward glances at the tree as they did so.

The reason was soon obvious, for as soon as the children and the two women had left the courtyard and gone into the house, the legs of a fourth child appeared as she stepped gingerly down off one of the upper branches. Soon he could see the rest of her and a squirming, pale brown puppy held under the child's right arm.

This was Rebecca.

Joseph asked, "May I hold the puppy for you while you get down?" And he went forward to her with his hands outstretched.

"Thank you," said Rebecca. "He's Timothy's puppy

really. Timothy thought he'd like to be taken up into the tree to look at the blossoms. But I don't think a dog feels very much at home in a tree, sir, do you?"

"No, my child." Joseph released the puppy on the ground and watched him dash off into the house with the others, a happy, wriggling little streak of eagerness.

For a moment Rebecca sat on the lower branch of the tree, the sun on her bright black hair and on her warm brown eyes. The red sprays of the carob blossoms waved in the wind behind her.

"Who are you?" she asked calmly.

"My name is Joseph."

"My name is Rebecca. I live in Bethsaida. That's a place that . . . oh, it's *far* away from here."

"Is it?" he asked.

"Did you come to see my father?"

"Not exactly. Your mother brought me here so I could talk to you, Rebecca."

She started to come down from the branch, but Joseph begged her to stay there.

"Please don't bother to come down, Rebecca. It suits you, sitting up there. And I could sit on this big round rock and talk to you."

"What about?"

"About you."

She nodded rather solemnly and smoothed her dusty small white dress as if she were receiving an ambassador.

Even her sandalled feet stayed still beneath the branch for a while. But since she continued to stare at him with a mixture of awe and respect and with some latent laughter in her eyes, he had to start the conversation on his own.

"It's a subject you may be tired of talking about," he said.

She nodded, smiling openly at last. "Did you come to ask what all the others ask?"

"What do they ask?"

" 'Tell us about the miracle, Rebecca! What was it like to be dead.' "

"You do sound rather tired of being asked."

"So would you be, sir."

"Probably I would because I don't have very much patience. But if I were to persist in asking what the others ask, Rebecca, what would you tell me, I wonder?"

She stared at him a moment longer, and then, "I'd tell you that as far as I know, sir, I was never dead at all!"

Clearly she was not making fun of him, or of herself either. Nor was she belittling the event. As far as she knew, she was clearly telling him the truth.

"What really happened, Rebecca?"

"I was quite sick, sir—terribly, awfully sick. It was so hard to breathe. I remember lying in bed at home, with mother and father there and when I was asleep I remember them talking about me—far, far away in the distance. They were talking to Aunt Hagar, who lives across the

MAN BEFORE THE MORNING

street, and they were saying I was in danger. Have you
ever been in danger?"

"Yes, indeed, I have. Perhaps almost as badly as you
were."

"Tell me."

"How about finishing your story first?"

She shook her head at that. "You first!" she demanded.

There was nothing to be gained by hurrying her. He
shifted his position on the smooth rock near her tree,
folding his hands across his knees as he did so.

"Long ago when I was a little boy, Rebecca, my father
and mother let me travel with them in a caravan. It was a
great big caravan with silks and scents and many camels.
My father was a merchant in Damascus and my mother
liked to travel with him every time she could."

"Is that when you were in danger, sir?"

"I was coming to that. When our caravan was about
half way between Damascus and Jerusalem, we were
attacked by mountain brigands. My father and mother
were killed, and I was badly wounded. They took the
camels and the treasure goods away. Perhaps they
thought they'd killed me too. Perhaps they didn't care;
they weren't afraid of a mere child. I think I was almost
dead. At least a part of me died then. Do you understand?
Until I found someone else. So you see I was in quite a lot
of danger. But why don't you tell me *your* story now?"

"There isn't much more to say. Except about Jesus."

"What about him?"

"He made me well again."

"Do you remember how?"

She looked at him and smiled again, then gazed above his head across the fields as if she were remembering.

"Do you remember my telling you about my father and mother and Aunt Hagar talking around my bedside far far down and away from me?"

"Yes, I do."

"Well, they didn't really do that very long, you know. Because it got very dark after a while. Well, not really dark but different. And Barnabas was sitting under a tree there, carving a reed flute for me. He used to be very good at that."

"Barnabas?"

"He was my brother."

"*Was* your brother?"

"He was twelve years older than me. He died a long time ago."

"I see. And then what happened?"

"Then quietly it grew light again and the light became so bright that . . . well, it was a happy kind of light! And somewhere in the distance I heard a new voice calling me. "Get up, my child!" it said. And there I was in bed again, with this stranger looking down at me. In the corner I could see my father with his arm around my mother, and three other men beside them, three men I'd never seen before. They looked so solemn as they stood there that I think I laughed at them."

"And what about the stranger? Was that Jesus?"

"I thought he was a bit like Uncle Thomas, but kinder than Uncle Thomas. All I remember is wanting to go out to play again. I never felt so happy, not in all my life! And I was so hungry! I think he must have realized this because he told them to give me something to eat. Mother made me some lentil broth and after that I had some bread and honey. And even cow's milk! It's quite a change from goat's milk, sir, if you've ever had any."

"Yes, I have, Rebecca."

"May I go into the house, please, and play with the others?"

"Of course you may. And I'll come and say good-bye to your mother, for I must go, too. I have to get to Arima-thea."

He stood up from the rock and held his arms out, lifting her gently down from the branch onto the ground beside him. She could not have been much lighter than his frail wife. Then he held her hand, and with a wonder growing in him led her happily toward the house.

CHAPTER
5

The door of the sleeping room was open, but Zuilmah and the steward Jubal, each carrying one end of a rolled-up rug under one arm, halted before they reached it and listened intently.

They could hear quite clearly the faint rasp of Drusilla's breathing as they stood there. But the sound, despite an edge of strain in it, was a regular one, and after a moment of listening Zuilmah gave a confident nod.

"She's still asleep," she whispered. "It's safe to take it in there now."

Under his breath Jubal muttered, "Better take our sandals off."

Following his example, Zuilmah kicked her sandals aside with long-practiced ease and edged them with the side of one foot against the wall. Then she exchanged a look of readiness with Jubal, and the two of them holding the rug more firmly went softly into the room.

Zuilmah looked at her mistress with the genuine warmth of concern, noting that at any rate her sleep seemed peaceful.

At another nod from Jubal she put down her end of the rug, timing the action with his own, and the two of them rolled it out across the polished floor not far from the end of the bed.

"It's beautiful!" Zuilmah whispered, and they both stood still to admire it. It was a splendid, just-completed rug ordered directly from Damascus by their master.

It was embroidered wool on wool in an intricate design of blue and gold and crimson-purple. It gave the room an extra depth of luxury and a touch of vivid splendor where a shaft of sunlight fell across its corner.

A look of awe spread over their faces as they stood there staring down on it for it must have cost a fortune.

Unthinkingly, her mind lost in its rich magnificence, Zuilmah murmured, "He ordered it last year, months before he knew she wouldn't be here to enjoy it with him very long. What a blessing it came in time!"

A slight movement, no more than the shifting of a coverlet, made Zuilmah turn abruptly to the bed. And what she saw brought a hand flying up to her mouth as if to stuff back into her mouth the words already spoken. Not only were they spoken, but from the look in the eyes of her mistress only too clearly heard.

Drusilla sat up painfully in bed, leaning heavily on an elbow. And while her bright, wide-open eyes were on Zuilmah, her lips were framing a question to which it was clear she had already guessed the answer. "What a blessing it came in time ... for *what*, Zuilmah?"

Zuilmah began to tremble, and the hand that had been over her mouth dropped down to clasp the other helplessly. "In time ... why, in time for Passover, mistress," she lied. And she knew how sharply the lie betrayed itself.

Drusilla shook her head, but still gazed at her handmaid with wide startled eyes. "You've been here in this house with me ever since I was a child, Zuilmah. When did you ever feel the need to lie to me—especially about something I already suspected?"

Zuilmah lowered her eyes. Jubal, looking from his mistress to Zuilmah then back again at Drusilla with a flood of pity in his eyes, bowed low, seeking a mute permission to withdraw. And Drusilla with the merest nod of understanding gave it.

He backed a step or two away, then left the chamber altogether.

Drusilla tried to sit a little more erect against her pillows. There was fear in the thrust of her chin, but she tried to soften her face for Zuilmah's sake. "You said your master ordered this new rug before he learned that I would not be here very long to share it with him."

Zuilmah stared, then slowly nodded.

"Do they believe I'm dying, Zuilmah?"

The question had been asked so simply that this time Zuilmah could not lie again, but neither could she answer immediately. She looked across the corner of the bed then sank to her knees in heavy-hearted helplessness, pressed her fingers to her eyes and started to sob.

Drusilla chided gently, "This is not serving me well! Tell me what you know about it."

Zuilmah nodded. Attempting to check her tears, she told her mistress woodenly but truthfully the little she knew. Yet the little held more of grim finality than Sosthenes himself might have betrayed with all the detail he could have added.

Drusilla listened to her handmaid's blunt recital with a kind of bright-eyed stillness. Once the words were spoken she looked as if she had withdrawn herself a thousand miles or more. Then she gazed slowly, achingly, about the room and at the view outside her window as if she were trying to clasp the long-familiar outlines ever closer.

At length with her face still averted, her pale cheeks catching a little of the warmer light of the late afternoon, she whispered, not intending to be listened to or overheard, 'O Lord Jehovah! Not when he needs me so!"

Then she turned to Zuilmah once again and tried to

stop the tremor in her voice as she spoke. "I haven't even looked at the new rug you just put down. Give me a hand so I can get a better look at it."

Zuilmah quickly got to her feet and went forward to her mistress, pulled back the coverlet and wrapped a shawl about her fragile shoulders. She placed one of her own strong arms so that Drusilla could lean all her slight weight on it as she swung over the edge of the bed.

With small determined steps Drusilla walked with Zuilmah's help to the end of the bed. There she hesitated for a moment, breathing heavily. Zuilmah helped her on to the rug itself. Her bare feet seemed to thrill at the touch of it, and the excitement brought an echo of her former strength into her voice. "How clearly I remember planning with your master to have this rug made, Zuilmah. It was early in the spring last year. Look how well those craftsmen in Damascus have woven it—in just the colors that we hoped for! Isn't it beautiful?"

"Yes, mistress."

Drusilla stared down at the rug with childlike joy. Then she stretched her free hand slightly down toward it. Without a word she sank to her knees. Zuilmah tried to steady her, believing at first that all her mistress sought to do was to touch the rich pile with her fingers.

Then she realized that something more was the matter.

"Help me back onto the bed, Zuilmah. The room is spinning round me...."

Zuilmah was frightened now. She tried to support her

101

mistress back along the edge of the bed, but Drusilla faltered, then suddenly fell face downward on the floor before Zuilmah could catch her.

At first the small form seemed so sickeningly still that Zuilmah held her breath. But she almost immediately realized that her mistress was still breathing. Indeed she was breathing so sharply and so desperately that Zuilmah knew her mistress was fighting to stay alive.

She shouted for the steward. "Jubal! Come here, Jubal! Quickly!"

Jubal hurried back into the room, his old eyes clearly fearful of what they might behold.

Tenderly, as her own father might, he lifted Drusilla back upon the bed. "She fainted," he said. "Get her some water. Nay, stay a moment and straighten out the pillows for her, Zuilmah. There, that's better. Now get the water."

"It's time the master was arriving." Zuilmah threw the words back from the door as if she felt that Joseph's homecoming could somehow solve the problem.

But Jubal looked at the closed eyes of Drusilla and shook his head. "I must go for Sosthenes," he said. "We mustn't wait until the master gets home."

* * * *

The two horsemen met where the road breasted the ridge over the village of Arimathea, Joseph riding his mount at a gentle trot and Jubal galloping with all the speed he could muster.

Joseph realized the moment he recognized his steward that only a crisis could have brought him up here like this. Were it not so, Jubal would have been riding one of the asses kept for household errands instead of one of his master's own fast horses.

Jubal did not waste any time. He poured out his story while one hand held the tugging reins and the other hand almost by force of habit made the quick, accustomed salutation.

"My mistress has been taken worse, sir. A little while ago she fainted. I think she may still be unconscious. I thought you'd wish me to get to Jerusalem as fast as I could for your physician."

"Of course. I'll go myself, Jubal. No, I must get back to her! She fainted?"

"She fell, sir; she's unconscious."

"Do you think. . . ?"

Jubal read the rest of the desperate question in his master's eyes and answered it. "She was breathing steadily, sir. Zuilmah's with her, and Anna was making some warm barley broth in the kitchen when I left."

Joseph was already swinging his horse to face the downward road into the village. "Let's not waste time," he called. "Bring the physician back with you, Jubal. Or better, let him ride ahead of you. His mount will be much

103

fresher. Tell him I'm waiting. Tell him. . . ." Joseph's last command was lost in the lunge of his horse down the road. He only heard like an echo of his thumping heart the galloping hoofs of Jubal's horse as they faded away into the dust of the Jerusalem road.

The rapid gallop of Joseph's horse helped stem the flood of sudden fear that threatened to engulf him. But the conflict that had been gathering force all through this journey home continued to grow and sharpen.

It had started with a picture he could not erase from his mind, the picture of Rebecca sitting on the branch of that carob tree with the blossoms waving in the sun behind her. And inseparable from that picture was the simple, honest echo of her voice—"I was quite sick, sir. Terribly, awfully sick. I could hardly breathe. . . ." And again her voice, brimming with life and eagerness: "Then quietly it grew light again. And the light became so bright . . . it was a happy kind of light! . . . I heard a new voice calling me. 'Get up, my child.' "

It was transparently clear that Rebecca had been telling him the truth, at least as far as she knew it. With equal clarity he had seen with his own eyes that she was made whole and well again. But all his life he had been taught to scorn such wild departures from the common realities of daily life. Such miracles were, of course, tricks of fancy brought on by swallowing the very heresies they said this Nazarene proclaimed.

Heresies?

MAN BEFORE THE MORNING

Another image now merged into the vivid picture his mind held of the child Rebecca, now, they said, brought back from the dead. It was the image of the Nazarene himself, tall and commanding, standing against one of the pillars in Solomon's Porch, wearing that plain white mantle with the well-worn traveling cloak thrown over it. He was saying incredible things to them, telling them he was the light of the world.

And yet ... no sharper words could tear a man apart as much at such a time as those two. And yet, was it possible that Jesus was right?

Who else, some woman in the crowd had asked, who else but the Messiah could speak with such authority that disease could vanish at his word?

And if, by some fantastic trick of time or history, this Jesus were indeed the true, the long-awaited one—if indeed this child of Jairus had been raised from the dead by him, then even the dying Drusilla....

The welter of such possible impossibilities brought nothing but a fresh confusion. How, he asked himself, could any reputable Sadducee indulge in such delusion? Or if he did indulge in them—if he, a Councillor of the great Sanhedrin, one of the ones chosen to convict Jesus, should turn in desperation to this very man—how could Drusilla, Malachi's daughter, help but resent and scoff at the act?

In inner turmoil Joseph spurred his horse into a faster gallop down the empty stretch of road that hugged the

105

ridge. The roofs of Arimathea were closer now, and beyond those roofs where the land began to climb again was home.

Joseph strained forward in the saddle, as if the extra inch might bring him there all the sooner. He tried to shape some sort of prayer, but prayer almost eluded him. Indeed the only prayer that rose in him came in the immemorial words of praise and homage that seemed more to mock than to comfort him. "Blessed be the glory of God!" were the words. Yet twice he repeated them, seeking God's word or will in them.

At last though he galloped through the outskirts of the village and up the road to the south of it. And at last he clattered into the stone-flagged courtyard of his home.

One of the stable boys, a lad called Caleb, ran forward to take the horse as Joseph sprang from it.

It was almost dark now. In the twilight the boy bowed quickly to his master in pity and respect. The gesture was as fleeting as it was wordless, but it was flooded with the compassion of one whose place it was to be silent for one whose place it was to command. Rushed though he was, Joseph got the message and gave the lad an answering nod of gratitude for it.

The fountain in the inner courtyard was not playing, having been turned off as usual at sunset. And there was no sound from the room beyond. Joseph strode over the marble floor, his footsteps echoing—it seemed enough to split the stillness of the night itself. He saw through the door of his sleeping room that Zuilmah was standing at the foot of the bed. And he saw, praise God, Drusilla lying back against her pillows, talking.

What she was saying he could neither hear nor tell, for at the sight of him she fell silent, losing her words in the relief of welcome.

In his relief he did not see the sudden dread that his arrival brought to Zuilmah. And her short, involuntary "Mercy on me, Master!" brought only a puzzled glance from him as he passed. Indeed, he was but barely conscious of her withdrawal from the room.

He flung off his short traveling cloak as he came up to the bedside, dropped on one knee and brought to his lips the hand Drusilla stretched toward him.

"You're feeling better!" he declared, kissed her fingertips again, and added, before she could reply to him, "I met Jubal on the road. By now he should have reached his destination. Sosthenes may even have begun his journey back."

"Did Jubal tell you what happened?"

Joseph closed his two warm hands over hers. "He said you'd fainted. Thank God you're looking more yourself again!"

With sudden earnestness she said, "I think you ought to know what caused it, Joseph. But you mustn't blame poor Zuilmah. I have suspected and would have found out soon enough in any case. I helped nurse my brother and mother, you know."

"Found out? What are you so concerned about?" he said, cold fear gripping him.

"Mostly about ... Joseph ..."—and this with a rush—"and what he will do when I'm not here to grumble at him any more!"

He froze. And though he saw it was not easy for her, she went on talking, making it all unalterably clear to him.

"Jubal and Zuilmah came in here this afternoon to put the new rug down, the one you ordered from Damascus. They thought I was asleep, and Zuilmah said how sad it was I wouldn't be here long to see it with you. Now you must tell me, Joseph, what Sosthenes told you about it. It is better if we don't hide these things from each other."

He looked at her with an ache in his throat, and he tried not to remember, yet remembered all the more, what Sosthenes had said: "she might just fold her hands and accept the end as cheerfully as she has accepted all the rest of her young life."

But he must be as honest with her now as she was being with him. "Sosthenes thinks there is danger, Drusilla. He warned us of the worst. But this, remember, is just the opinion of Sosthenes. I didn't say it was my own. And there are other doctors...."

She started coughing again, and the attack appeared to weaken her. When the spell was over her voice was scarcely audible, but as he mopped the perspiration from her brow, he heard her saying she must try to sleep now. She begged him to stay close beside her for a while, to let her hold his hand so she would know he was there.

"I'm here beside you!" he assured her gently. "As near as you are to yourself!" And then he settled himself, his hands still on hers, to wait for Sosthenes.

* * * *

About two hours later yet another man was hurrying down the road from Jerusalem toward the village of Arimathea. He was intent on making the best time his mount could manage, for the message he bore for Joseph was twofold, and was doubly urgent.

The fine, big Muscat ass was strong and all but tireless, as indeed he would have to be to carry a man the weight and size of Nicodemus. But he was as obstinate a beast as most of the rest of his kind, and this night Nicodemus could not easily contain his impatience with the creature.

The night was clear and cool, and the stars were all sharp and glittering above him. The scent of the wild hyssop and the more spicy camomile was already in the air, even though it was but the week of Passover with the harvesting of herbs still quite a time ahead.

But Nicodemus wasn't thinking about the beauty of nature. He wondered instead how best to give the needed

109

warning and make the necessary plea at the same time. Timid by nature, he also wondered just how far to go in saying what he had to say to this adopted son of the Lord Treasurer, for Malachi was a Sadducee of Sadducees.

As for his opinion of Joseph himself, though, Nicodemus had been aware of a growing admiration for the younger man ever since his elevation to the Council. There had indeed developed a community of interest that had in all probability surprised the two of them, for Nicodemus was a liberal-minded Pharisee, and Joseph by his very upbringing was inevitably a most conservative-minded Sadducee.

They had had arguments, of course. They had voted differently on many a measure enacted by the Sanhedrin. Some common honesty of purpose, though, in a group where such a virtue was not widely evident had drawn the two together on many a weighty matter. Because of Nicodemus' timidity and an aristocratic reticence on the part of Joseph, they had not yet presumed to fully explore the matter of their convictions. But a kinship had sprung up that led them to expect support from one another in the Council and had, incidentally brought them to the regular use of adjoining seats in the Council chamber.

Nicodemus had been to his friend's house in Arimathea before, and Drusilla had come to enjoy the older man's company. But it had been a long time since Nicodemus had visited them, because he had known of Drusilla's sickness for some time and had shared some of Joseph's anxiety over it.

Nicodemus remembered the names of Joseph's servants, even though in the past he had met them so fleetingly. And they, of course, remembered and respected him.

He knew that something unusual was happening the moment he rode into the outer courtyard, for a stranger's fine Arabian horse was tethered there. Also when Jubal came forward to help him dismount and tend his own mount, the steward had detached himself from a whispering knot of servants at the door of the kitchen quarters—Caleb and Anna, and Drusilla's handmaid, Zuilmah. The knot had broken up on his arrival.

Nicodemus pushed back the hood of his cloak and gave the steward a friendly smile. "Greetings, Jubal. How goes it with your master? I need to speak with him, and speedily."

"Greetings, my lord Nicodemus. My master's closeted with the physician, and with my mistress there," he nodded toward the inner courtyard and the closed door beyond it. "I've only just gotten back here from Jerusalem myself, sir. The physician came ahead of me."

"What's the matter, Jubal?"

"My mistress has taken a turn for the worse, sir. There's been a great deal of anxiety."

The Councillor shook his head, his own retiring nature

urging him to turn again and go back to Jerusalem, leaving these people to their own concern, his mission unaccomplished. But the matter was too urgent for that.

Jubal spoke again. "My master asked me, sir, not to disturb him. But if you'll go into the inner courtyard and be seated there, I'll bring you some wine and let him know you're here. And I'll see that Caleb feeds your ass and waters him. I hope you won't have long to wait."

Nicodemus gave the steward his traveling cloak and let him take his mount away. Then he walked into the inner courtyard and sat beneath one of the lantern-bearing sconces on the further wall—about as far away from the closed door as he could, as if to emphasize his great reluctance to disturb their privacy.

Almost immediately Jubal returned with the flagon of wine, poured him a goblet and left him. Nicodemus did not have long to wait, for presently the door of the sleeping room opened and Sosthenes came out followed by Joseph.

Nicodemus rose to his feet, but did not move toward them. He was, however, a big man and it was inevitable that he should be noticed.

Joseph turned at once and recognizing Nicodemus excused himself to Sosthenes, then crossed the courtyard toward his colleague.

The older man had never seen his friend so pale and

troubled, and even Joseph's customary smile was nothing more than the momentary lifting of a shadow from his face.

"There's trouble here, my friend," he said. "But I will talk with you as soon as Sosthenes has gone. You must forgive me while I speak with him alone a moment. We couldn't do so in there with Drusilla awake."

Nicodemus yearned to say some words of reassurance, but all he did was nod his understanding. And Joseph turning quickly walked away to Sosthenes again, and the two of them stood talking in a low voice. But there was an obvious tension in the air, and from the bits of information that Nicodemus was able to overhear he concluded that Sosthenes felt there was no more hope and that Joseph was planning on consulting someone else. Nicodemus looked away with fresh anxiety in his eyes, and wondered how he could add fresh worry to the increased burden his friend was now carrying.

Joseph and the physician did not talk long though, and as they came out of the courtyard Sosthenes raised his arm in a farewell salutation to the Councillor as he passed. Joseph returned to Nicodemus.

"Drusilla's very drowsy," he said quietly, "and I hope she'll sleep a little now. I must try not to disturb her. Sit here beside me, Nicodemus, where I can hear her call if she should need me."

113

MAN BEFORE THE MORNING

At Joseph's suggestion Nicodemus sat on the semicircular seat by the edge of the fountain pond, and his friend sat almost facing him.

"What about Drusilla?" Nicodemus asked as if he didn't know. "What did the physician have to say?"

"He had already said we couldn't hope to save her. But she didn't know that, not until today. Now that she's found out about it, well, he still maintains there's nothing more he can do. And he implied it might be easier for Drusilla and for all of us if we didn't have to wait much longer."

Joseph read the question on the face of Nicodemus and answered it quite simply. "In the next few days, he thinks."

Something seemed to come into the Pharisee's eyes that he ached to say but could not. Instead he murmured, "May God comfort you!"

A sudden restlessness appeared to seize Joseph, and he stood up again, much agitated. He took a step or two away, only to come back again immediately. He appeared to be turning something over in his mind. As he stared down at the seated Nicodemus he seemed to reach the decision that the risk was worth taking.

"I don't know what has brought you, Nicodemus, but it can't be more important than the question I am going to ask you."

"What brought me here concerns your life, Joseph. And another's life."

Joseph stretched an eloquent hand toward the door of

the sleeping room. "What I want to ask concerns her life, Nicodemus."

Joseph paused there, and Nicodemus bridged his hesitation with a smile. It prodded Joseph forward.

"Nicodemus, from what you've said in the Sanhedrin of this Jesus of Nazareth, I've come to the conclusion you must know much more than you've said. I've started to believe that, Councillor or not, and for that matter Pharisee or not, you've set yourself apart from this conspiracy that's building up against him. You seem to be as repelled as I am about this drive for his destruction. Am I right on this?"

Nicodemus stared across at him with caution. Joseph's voice grew sharper.

"Death doesn't wait for men to fence with secrets, Nicodemus. You've come to me in need. I am in need already. If you have any knowledge of this ... this man from Nazareth, then tell me where he's staying in Jerusalem. I beg you, Nicodemus, tell me where to find him!"

The Pharisee's last hurdle of reserve dissolved. "Joseph, it was about this Jesus that I came to talk to you," he said simply.

Joseph sat down again, watching his friend closely. "Up in Bethphage today, Nicodemus, I saw a child they say this man brought back from the dead! I met the little girl and talked with her. And in my heart I half came to believe the tale, even while my head was saying no to it.

There could have been no reason in the world for them to lie to me. The mother and child were telling me the truth, at any rate as far as they perceived it."

"As far as they perceived it?"

Joseph nodded, twisting one hand quite sharply in the other. "You're right to chide me, Nicodemus. More of my reservations, I suppose you're thinking. I've no time left for reservations. Do you believe . . ." and Joseph leaned a hand across, gripping the other's forearm with a sudden earnestness, "Do you believe this Nazarene could heal Drusilla? Would she have to be his follower first? Have you ever heard of his going to the house of anyone who's not one of his own?"

Nicodemus nodded. "He calls for faith, Joseph, but I know he healed a Centurion's son. And just before he started on this journey here, they say he healed a Canaanite. He's lifted many out of much confusion—including, among the doubters, a Pharisee you know, a man who had a tremendous burden on his mind."

"A Pharisee?"

"Me!" The sudden smile was utterly sincere, and Joseph felt a rush of fellow-feeling for the man, knowing that for Nicodemus to admit this thing at all, and to admit it to a fellow Councillor of the Sanhedrin, was to risk his reputation. And possibly much more than that.

"Do you believe in him?"

"I do."

MAN BEFORE THE MORNING

Joseph stood up again, and started pacing to and fro, then swung abruptly round. "I want to get to him, Nicodemus! How much I can believe I just don't know. But if there's a chance, even if there's only a chance in a thousand, I've got to seize it. I've got to get to him before it's all too late."

"Yes, of course. But there's something else I've got to tell you. I hurried down here from Jerusalem because the hours are running out for him!"

"For Jesus?"

Nicodemus nodded, then asked in almost a whisper, "And possibly for you, my friend."

"What do you mean?"

"I came to ask you a favor. And since what I ask depends a lot upon your safety, let me start with you. Or rather, let me start with Zibeon."

"With Zibeon?" Joseph was rigid now and listening tensely.

"Zibeon had you followed in Bethphage, Joseph! Why or how he's come to think you're having dealings with the followers of Jesus I don't know. I think that crafty Ephraim's at the bottom of it. And from gossip I heard from Rahab, who was in his cups again, I gather there is nothing Zibeon would stop at to discredit you. He'd well like to be rid of you."

"This I already know."

"Why does he hate you so strongly?"

MAN BEFORE THE MORNING

Joseph stared at Nicodemus for some seconds, stiff with caution. Then he threw whatever he had left of reticence overboard and spoke not just as man to man, but as friend to friend.

"Answering that could cost my life, Nicodemus. But obviously you trust me, so I'm going to trust you."

Nicodemus gestured to the marble seat for Joseph to sit, but Joseph remained standing.

"Months ago," he said, "I discovered Zibeon breaking a law for which the penalty is death. As Councillor I was duty-bound to report the thing to the Sanhedrin. Instead I kept my peace. And I could be stoned to death because I did."

"What did Zibeon do?"

"He made a fortune out of a Roman soldier's wager. One of the captains from the Antonia fortress, a man with a lot more wealth behind him than his pay, wagered with his friends up there that he could get into the Temple without this profanation being discovered. He vowed to get beyond the Court of the Gentiles into the Court of the Priests, and then up the steps of the altar itself!"

The gasp from Nicodemus was loud enough to bring a moment's pause to Joseph's tale. Then he went on with it.

"It was Zibeon's turn that day to supervise the incense for the altar. And he allowed this Roman on payment of a minor fortune to change into the vestments of a priest. He made it possible for the man to come through the last

118

barrier and mount the very steps of the altar! And a couple of Roman witnesses, also appropriately disguised, watched from some distance off in the Court of the Men."

"Oh God, have mercy on us! How did you discover this?"

"One of the watching Romans—but that's another story, and there's no time for it. I met with Zibeon alone after that, and charged him with the crime. At first he tried to lie and bluster his way out of it as you might expect, but suddenly he went to pieces. He entreated me to keep his secret even though he knew that in doing so I'd be breaking the law myself. But because of Zibeon's father, and a pressing need for him to support the old man, I said I would agree to this. But of course I've told no one else about it."

"But what about the wager money?"

"Do you remember the Temple Treasury receiving a windfall in the month of Kislev? That's your answer."

Nicodemus threw a hand up to his chin, visibly shaken. "If this be so," he said, "then surely Zibeon would want to keep his distance from you!"

"I know too much for Zibeon's safety. If I were dead, the danger of discovery disappears. But I'm too highly placed to take hasty action. Too many risks, you know. And so he bides his time."

"But Zibeon himself belongs to the Sanhedrin!"

"Let's not deceive ourselves, Nicodemus! Violence does

not die within a man because he has taken a vow to the Sanhedrin! No, Zibeon's been nursing thoughts like this against me for quite a time. He's just as cunning as his wily Ephraim. And he's ambitious. So what could satisfy him better than to expose an enemy within the Council's membership itself?"

"I can't believe it. And yet I do believe it."

"I'm not afraid of him, Nicodemus. In any case, he's waiting till he can be absolutely sure of me. That's why he had me followed to Bethphage. And anyway he's very much afraid of Malachi, my foster father."

Nicodemus shook his head as if the weight of all these revelations was too much for him.

But Joseph turned again toward the inner room, his head aslant, listening intently. Satisfied after a moment that Drusilla was not calling him, he turned back to Nicodemus. By now he was less tense and strained, as if unburdening himself had eased him in mind and body.

"What did you want of me, Nicodemus?"

"First I wanted to warn you about Zibeon and urge you to look behind you when you go abroad these next few days. But more important I wanted to beg you to lift your voice with mine while there may still be time to stop this travesty of justice that is building up against Jesus!"

"What do you know of it?"

Nicodemus glanced around the courtyard automatically, even though he knew his spoken word was safe. Nonetheless he spoke so much more quietly that Joseph had to strain to hear him.

"Something devilish is afoot, something less obvious than naming a fresh delegation to lay another snare for him. What it is I can't discover. And Mordecai who can usually be counted on for information is as silent as a sepulchre about it."

"How do you know of it?"

"One of the Nazarene's own group of disciples was closeted with Caiaphas today. I heard that this man—his name is Judas, I believe—came with some plan to talk about."

"Are you afraid just because you are a follower of Jesus?"

Nicodemus looked squarely up at that, directly into Joseph's face. "Not just because of that, but because there's already been too much false witnessing. Of all the men around me in the Chamber of Hewn Stone I think that only you would fight for any common honesty in such a thing. And I've a feeling more's at stake in this than any of us realize. I also think...."

Joseph held up a hand for silence. In the brief pause they heard the faint sound of Drusilla's coughing.

"I must get back to her, Nicodemus. And this time I must stay with her a while. One thing I'll promise you. I will be honest with you. Honest whatever happens. You may trust me about Jesus. Before you go, tell me where I can find him."

Nicodemus had risen to his feet. He nodded understandingly. "I think he's up in Bethany," he said. "Ask for him in the house of Lazarus, the olive grower."

"In Bethany," Joseph repeated, already turning away. "In the house of Lazarus. Thank you, Nicodemus."

Joseph walked quietly off into the sleeping room, so preoccupied he did not notice the sound of the older man's footsteps as they faded away through the outer courtyard.

There was no violent spell of coughing this time. Perhaps the strain was eased a little for Drusilla by the sight of him, for as he moved into the circle of the lamplight she realized how glad she was to see him again.

She stretched a hand to him, but fell back on the pillows as if that simple action had exhausted her.

"I didn't even know I'd been asleep," she said. "Today's been such a long one. Is it still the same day?"

"Yes, my love. And I think that in the kitchen Anna's still quite busy making preparations for the Passover. Just as she was when Sosthenes was here."

"The Passover! I'd almost forgotten it. I'm so ashamed there's nothing I can do about it. If only...."

He smiled at her, placing a gentle finger of reproof across her lips and shaking his head at her. "Let's not concern ourselves about it. There's something else I have to talk about. It's something very important."

She turned her eyes to him expectantly, and he saw an ache in them that told him how very much these moments mattered to her.

"Drusilla, you know what Sosthenes said. But even though he is a skilled physician, one of the best we know, his word is not the only one to rest on. There is another man I want to try to bring here to you."

"Another physician?"

"Some might call him that."

"Who is he?"

He hesitated but the barest moment. Then he knew that no matter how she felt about it, there could be no turning back.

"Jesus of Nazareth," he said.

She looked up, startled, and tried to raise herself up on an elbow. "Do you really mean this?"

He nodded. "I think these tales of him may not be quite as fanciful as we've believed, Drusilla. I've spoken to a child whom they declared had died. You should have seen how well she was. You should have heard her laughing! And Nicodemus says there have been many more...."

She had looked away from him, and when she spoke with her face still averted, there was a tremor in her voice. "That's absurd. You're becoming too distraught. Father says there is much danger in the man."

"Your father doesn't always understand, dear love! Nor will he always listen." He gently clasped her shoulders with his hands, turning her round to him.

"This Jesus could hardly be more dangerous than the risk of losing you, Drusilla. I want to go for him. And I think I know where to find him. Nicodemus says he is in Bethany. I want to get him to come back here with me!"

She studied him and, as she looked, appeared to see right through him. And at last she said something that seemed so strange to him that he in turn was startled.

"It isn't just Jesus you want to find, Joseph. It's yourself! For weeks you've been aching to find some peace of mind again, some of the confidence you've lost since you became a Councillor. Or perhaps it isn't yourself you're looking for either. Perhaps the one you're trying to find is God."

"I never told you. . . ."

"To love a man is usually to watch a man. Women seldom tell all they see."

"But it is for you."

"Of course it's for me! And I know how much of a struggle you must have had to want to take so wild a chance for me! I also know that if the Council knew of it you'd still defy them. In the end you've always done what you've believed to be right, Joseph. Half of you longs to believe in this man Jesus because you are lost and afraid.

124

Half of you already thinks he can heal me, just as you say he's healed so many others. But half-beliefs have never been enough to satisfy my husband."

He shook his head, troubled by the weakness in her voice. "Drusilla, if only I can get him here ... if I can bring him to you."

"Go for him then. But tell him, if you find him, that I have little faith in him. I'll assent to this on one condition. Make me a promise, Joseph."

"Of course I will."

"Promise that you won't come back to me before you've either found him, or found peace about him!"

Looking closely at her, he began to see a little of the cost to her of getting him to give her such a promise. Perhaps she was sending him away so he wouldn't have to witness her passing. He closed his eyes in doubt and desperation, then he looked quite steadily at her. "I'll promise that," he said.

She slowly nodded, as if it were a compact she alone could understand. At length she said, "But you must rest before you go. Get up before the dawn and ride in early if you must. But first you must have sleep."

"And you need sleep, Drusilla. I will not waken you in the dark when I go."

She let him set her back upon her pillows. But when he stooped to kiss her and say goodnight he felt her fingers clutch him tightly, as tightly as she could. It was as if for all her fine, brave words, she was a child again, a child afraid of the dark.

* * * *

Before sunrise he was out along the road toward Jerusalem.

It was the day before the Passover. And even before he joined the masses who would be traveling toward the Holy City, he knew this would be no ordinary pilgrimage.

The purple of pre-dawn began to melt at last into the day. There was a vastness now in the changing sky, a vastness he had not realized before this morning.

Intuitively he knew danger lay ahead of him. But there was more within this day than danger. He tried to shake this awesome premonition. He even succeeded for a time, for as he crossed the Kidron at last and took the winding road to Bethany, it was only of Drusilla that he thought and of the way her hands had clutched him.

CHAPTER
6

Though the road wound slowly to the east, rising and dipping in the folds of Olivet, he found himself continually climbing higher, resting his horse as much as he could on the steeper inclines and moving in the main directly into the sun.

Today it was a busy road, with nearly all its travelers going in the opposite direction past him down toward Jerusalem.

Most were in groups and mounted on donkeys or mules, or occasionally horseback. And some, particularly those who hailed from a distance, were spread out down the road on strings of camels.

They came not just from villages in easy reach but from the heat and dust of Jericho, up from the valley of the

127

Jordan, out of the arid wastes of Ammon and the plains of Gilead. And here and there among the simple clothes of farming folk who lived but a few hours journey hence were feminine gleams of silk and gold brocade, of soft, embroidered veils from lands as far afield as Persia. But upon their faces was a common eagerness, the annual excitement of this holiest of all the holy festivals.

There was a morning breeze across the uplands now, blowing not just the scent of balsams across the road but also the sounds of the ancient psalms the travelers were singing, the psalms that had been sung each Passover since the days of David:

> *I was glad when they said unto me, Let us go into the house of the Lord.*
> *Our feet shall stand within thy gates,*
> *O Jerusalem. . . .*
> *Whither the tribes go up, the tribes of the Lord,*
> *unto the testimony of Israel, to give thanks unto the name of the Lord.*

There was a fervor in their faces. Joseph felt the faith that inspired them on this warm spring morning was the same strong faith that must have shone upon and from them in the journey to the Promised Land itself. Looking at them he felt he was looking back to the beginning of the nation's story. He heard again what Moses had proclaimed: "The Lord will pass through to smite the

MAN BEFORE THE MORNING

Egyptians, and when he seeth the blood upon the lintel, and on the two side posts, the Lord will pass over the door, and will not suffer the destroyer to come into your houses to smite you."

Few were the faces that seemed touched as yet by the corruption that was spreading nowadays outwards from Jerusalem. The fountain of their exaltation still sprang sharp and clear in their eyes. And despite the growing problems that afflicted them—the taxes that burdened them and the spawning of fresh laws-within-the-Law that had begun to eat into their freedom—their songs were clearly heartfelt. Their sense of wonder as they looked down on Jerusalem was unfeigned.

Looking at them as he passed, Joseph remembered it was among such men and women, aye, and among such children too, that the Nazarene, himself a countryman, was held to have performed his deeds. Jesus must have come from Jericho along this selfsame road, and was still, Joseph hoped, in the home of Mary and Martha, in the village whose scattered houses now began to rise on either side of him.

A vigorous-looking woman, erect despite her graying hair, was walking almost parallel with him across a cultivated patch of ground that edged the road, her thin arms holding a pitcher of water on her head.

Joseph hailed her and she turned toward him and halted as he reined his horse and drew closer.

"I'm looking for the house of Lazarus, the olive grower," he said. "The one who has a sister Mary and another sister Martha."

The woman glanced with momentary curiosity, noting the horse and taking in perhaps the richness of his cloak. And he felt there was a suspicious note in her attitude. Her voice was affable enough though and she turned her chin toward the top of the sloping field up which she was walking.

"It's the house that stands the furthest back," she said, "the second one when you come to the bend in the road."

He thanked her and hurried up the road, a quickening excitement in him, a tightening of his hand upon the rein. It was a pleasant-looking house, with its walls and wide flat roof baked honey-cream and copper by the sun. Broad fig trees hugged it close enough upon the side that faced him to throw their dappled shadows over it. And there were doves about the place.

But as Joseph rode his horse into the open courtyard there were no people or animals in sight, nor sandals at the door.

His intuition told him he was too late, that any guests had long departed. But as he reined his horse and dismounted, he tried to restrain this misgiving. He was glad to see a woman come up to him from a little garden at the side.

She was quite young and wore a plain blue woolen

130

chiton with a soft white veil. It blew aside a little as she moved, letting the sun shine on her long, dark hair. She had a shallow basket filled with some greens she had just been gathering.

Joseph bowed, and was immediately conscious of the fact that though she smiled politely at him she watched him very guardedly.

"I hope this is the house of Lazarus, the olive grower," he said, and since she did not answer him immediately, he went on rather clumsily, "the house of Lazarus and his sisters, Mary and Martha."

"I am Mary," she said simply.

"Lady," he said, "I've come from Arimathea in search of Jesus of Nazareth."

She shook her head emphatically. "He is not here," she said, and sounded relieved that she could tell him so.

"A friend told me he was staying in this house."

There was still fear and some degree of caution in her eyes. He knew that his horse and the clothes he wore betrayed his wealth.

"I have been on the road from Arimathea since long before dawn," he said. "I came to beg him to come back with me."

"To Arimathea?"

"To heal my wife."

The honest ring of Joseph's words appeared to dissolve the fear in her eyes.

"You must be thirsty, sir, after your journey. Come in with me and let me give you some water."

He tied his horse to a stake by the door and went with her into the simple room beyond.

Another woman was there, at work at the kitchen table.

She was a slightly older, plumper, brown-haired woman with a ready smile on her face. She looked up from the wooden bowl over which she was bending, and there was an honest curiosity in her eyes.

"This is my sister Martha," Mary said. "She's making the *haroseth* for our Passover. Martha, the gentleman has come in search of Jesus. His wife is sick."

"My name is Joseph," he said with a slight bow, then gave a grateful smile as Mary handed him a goblet of cold water from the jar on the stone floor.

"I've heard about your brother Lazarus," he added.

"He left quite early this morning to go to the Temple," Martha volunteered. "You must have passed him on the road."

"I hoped I'd have a chance to meet him. I'd like to ask him. . . ." He hesitated, but Mary put him at his ease.

"About the miracle? That's what so many others come up here to ask about. They want to find out for themselves if it is true. I think my brother's getting a bit tired of it all."

"That's very understandable. Has Jesus also gone down to the Temple in Jerusalem?"

The sisters glanced at one another in momentary

hesitation, but Mary, turning back to study him, seemed satisfied with what she saw and she said frankly, "He left before daybreak with some of his disciples."

"For the Temple?"

"I don't know." It was more than a simple negation. There was a need for protection behind it, and something about that need communicated itself to Joseph too. There was fear in Mary's eyes again, and Joseph, remembering what Nicodemus had said, asked with new concern, "Do you know if his disciple Judas was with him when he left?"

The effect of the name was instantaneous. Mary shook her head, and clasping her hands in front of her, pressed them against each other in misgiving.

"Why did you speak of Judas?" she asked quickly, and he knew at once that he should not have named the man. Nor could he tell her what he had heard from Nicodemus.

"I think this Judas is a man to be watched," he said lamely.

"I am ... I am afraid because of him," said Mary in a whisper. And Martha stopped her work, watching her sister with obvious anxiety.

"I don't know you, sir," said Mary. "I pray you come here as a friend."

"I came to ask the help of Jesus for my wife," he repeated earnestly, and wished with all his heart that he had left at once, as he now must do.

The sisters nodded. "Sir," said Mary, "Jesus said strange

and terrible things about this day. If you should see him, guard him well!"

Martha, placing a finger on her lips, threw her sister a look of warning. And Joseph took his leave of them, only too well aware again, much more clearly now, of the mounting danger in the air.

* * * *

Dusk was about to fall when Nicodemus got back from the Sanhedrin to his house in the Street of the Vintners. And though it was a clear and beautiful twilight that had fallen on Jerusalem, as if to show the city off to the thousands still approaching for the Passover, it was a strange, uneasy night that was beginning.

Nicodemus felt lonely. Unlike most of the other members of the Council he lived by himself, with an active and esteemed old manservant, Shuah, to look after him.

This year his kinsfolk, because of the advancing years of his sister, would keep the Passover where most of them now lived, far to the south in Hebron. It was hard for him because it was at Passover time a man most missed his kin. The Law indeed demanded that he should be with his family for the feast, and it was only the pressure of his service on behalf of the Law that had permitted him to ask for and obtain permission not to journey to Hebron to join the others.

134

MAN BEFORE THE MORNING

It was not just loneliness, however, that shadowed this particular nightfall for Nicodemus. It was a growing awareness, more frightening because of its very vagueness, that tonight was the night that had been chosen for some final action against Jesus of Nazareth.

The matter should, of course, have been the concern of the whole Sanhedrin. Yet not even the twelve of the High Council had been told. Not one of them, as far as he had been able to ascertain, had been given any details by Caiaphas of the plot Nicodemus was convinced was now afoot.

Such secrecy was typical, for Caiaphas preferred to hand his colleagues an accomplished fact, trusting only such intimates as he could count on to follow him blindly. And their number had been steadily decreasing.

Here in his own house Nicodemus had just washed his feet and hands in the water Shuah had poured out for him. Now he reclined on the couch that had been drawn up to a low table.

It was a very simple meal that Shuah served him—salted fish and barley bread, with a flagon of wine, followed by fresh sycamore figs and a few dates brought in from the fruit market.

Tonight, though, Shuah went about his duties without his customary cheerfulness. By habit he was correct and unobtrusive, but usually there was a measure of warm-hearted give-and-take between the two. Tonight he was quite obviously ill at ease, and his anxiety concerned his master for whom he would gladly suffer and to whose welfare he had grown thoroughly devoted. It was in fact his master who had first spoken to him of the Nazarene, and after some seeking-out and humble listening on Shuah's part, a growing wonder and conviction concerning this same Jesus was now a secret that master and servant had in common.

As Shuah tipped the flagon to refill his master's goblet, Nicodemus questioned him. "Something's troubling you today, Shuah. What is it?"

Shuah hesitated for a moment, and then, "I've been expecting word from Malchus, sir."

"Malchus?"

"The High Priest's servant, sir."

Nicodemus looked up sharply. "Why should he be sending any message here?"

"After I got to know him better, Master, he began to confide in me that he had begun to believe in the Nazarene as ... as we do, sir. He cannot leave the side of Lord Caiaphas, of course, but I believe he thinks some evil deed is to be done this night. He said he would endeavour to get word to us. I am very much afraid though, Master, lest you should get too much involved in this."

"Involved? You should be ashamed to mention the word, Shuah! What would have happened to so many of

136

those helpless people if the Nazarene had stopped to wonder if he ought to get involved with them?"

It was clear that Shuah felt the weight of the rebuke, but it was just as clear how much concerned he was.

"I fear your life itself may be in peril, sir."

"And what of the peril to his life? What of...." Nicodemus got no further, for a sharp, insistent knocking at the door froze the sentence on his lips and made him swing around. Shuah hurried to open it.

It was no messenger from Malchus. It was Joseph who stood there, sharp-etched in the moonlight.

Shuah backed into the room and opened the door wide as he did so. Joseph strode forward wearily. "Thank God you are home, Nicodemus! You're probably one of the very few who know where I might find him."

"Come and sit down, Joseph. You look exhausted."

Joseph gratefully sank into the seat that Shuah placed for him. A moment's caution had gripped Nicodemus. "You think I'm one of the few who know where you might find whom, Joseph?"

"You well know whom I mean! You told me in my house that I might find him up in Bethany."

Nicodemus scanned his friend's face carefully. "By any chance did the Council send you here, or do you come on your own?"

"I come on my own, of course. I got to Bethany too late, Nicodemus. I've sought him all day long. I waited in the

Temple, walked up and down in Solomon's Porch for hours on end, followed a dozen useless leads."

There was no mistaking the earnestness in Joseph's voice, and Nicodemus was satisfied.

"I only wish I could tell you, Joseph. I'd give a lot to know where he might be just now. I haven't any notion. The city's swallowed him, and his disciples with him. I think Jerusalem's more crowded now than it has ever been."

"I must get to him."

"To try to take him down to Arimathea, to see Drusilla? You must have realized by now there's very little chance...."

"It isn't just that, Nicodemus." Joseph paused there and was glad to drink the goblet of wine Shuah offered him. While he did so, Nicodemus pressed his point.

"Then what is it? Why aren't you on your way back to Arimathea where she lies waiting for you?"

Joseph heard the question with distress, and over the brim of the goblet he closed his eyes in a moment's desperation.

He knew what kind of an answer Nicodemus sought, yet fought against giving it. The fruitlessness of the long day's wait, the gathering sense of portent in it all—these things had done strange things to him. Amazed at himself, yet with no strain or artificiality, he heard himself begin to voice these things.

"I want to get to him, Nicodemus, because I feel in some incredible way that he needs me. He's in danger and I feel I may be able to help. Perhaps this all sounds unbelievable to you. I know it does to me. But if I try to push it from my mind as just a bit of tired imagination, the sense of being needed only grows the sharper."

"I can't explain it either, but I sense something too."

Joseph hesitated, aware that the servant Shuah had now gone to his own quarters in the house and that he was alone with Nicodemus.

"Back in Arimathea," he said presently, "you said you had a feeling more was at stake in this than any of us realized. Today is proving it for me."

"How?"

"I've talked to many men and women throughout the day about him—beginning with that Mary of Bethany who sheltered him last night. And many others. Ordinary people touched by extraordinary faith. Little by little, voice by voice, I've started to realize that it's all true, Nicodemus! It's true, this power and glory we've been hearing of! People have been healed. People have been raised!"

"And Drusilla?"

Joseph turned away, pressing a hand to his chin as if the little pressure might ease the mental tension that was troubling him. "I can't tell you, Nicodemus. I can't tell you. And I can't explain it. Having Drusilla healed would mean as much as life to me! Yet I believe the life of this Galilean stranger is growing vital to the lot of us—to you, to me, to Drusilla. How a total stranger can make me feel like this I just can't tell you. Do I sound like someone mouthing riddles?"

"Perhaps like a man who starts to see the answers to the riddles."

"I hope to God that's so."

Nicodemus drew a little closer, as if to share more fully what he had to say.

"My friend," he said, "I too once sought out this man by night. I find myself remembering many times the things he said to me. Once he said something I've never forgotten: 'God so loved the world that he gave his only begotten son, that whoever should believe in him'—*whoever* should believe in him, Joseph—'should not perish, but have everlasting life.' I didn't believe it. It didn't make sense. Now I begin to grasp the fringe of it at last!"

As Joseph listened there was yet another knock at the door, and Shuah came out from the back of the house and crossed to answer it. Whoever stood there, however, did not come in, but was both breathless and brief.

Even though Nicodemus and Joseph did not see him the man appeared to be known to Shuah. "Malchus sends you a message, Shuah," said the man. "He says 'the trap is to be sprung in the garden of Gethsemane.'"

They could hear the gasp of astonishment from Shuah. "When?" he asked.

"Tonight. They're already on their way there."

"But...."

"I mustn't stand here. I must get back to the house before the porter finds out I left."

"Who is on the way to Gethsemane?"

"The High Priest and some of the Council, and all the Temple Guard they could get hold of, to say nothing of the rabble following after them. I must get back...."

It seemed that as quickly as he had come the stranger left and Nicodemus, who had stood up and was about to reach the door, failed even to set eyes on him.

"You heard him, Master?"

Nicodemus nodded. He had already reached for his head-cloth from a peg beside the door, and was now tying it above his forehead. "I must go after them, Joseph. I must try to reach Gethsemane before it's too late. Even if only one member of the Sanhedrin can raise a voice against this madness, it may prevent it."

"You mean if two men do so, Nicodemus. I'm coming with you."

"Good. We may well need each other."

"And he may need both of us." Joseph felt at last that now he could move and act, that this might be the role he was to play to save the Nazarene.

MAN BEFORE THE MORNING

Nicodemus led the way out into the street without stopping for more talk. Joseph followed closely, with Shuah staying behind and looking with anxiety at his master. He reluctantly backed inside again and closed the door.

Joseph and Nicodemus talked little as they made their way through the crowded streets. The urgency was too palpable for that, and the crowds of pilgrims, almost as thick as they had been through the day despite the fact that night had fallen, were but so many obstacles blocking their way.

At length they were out of the city though and over the Kidron. The crowds had thinned a little on the way, but here in the grove of olive trees known as Gethsemane it was already clear that something new and different was afoot.

They found themselves indeed on the heels of a motley throng of people following a serpentine line of torches just ahead of them.

Joseph and Nicodemus quickened their pace. Soon they had not only succeeded in getting into the fringe of the ragged crowd, but had elbowed their way through it to such good purpose that they at last began to overtake the torch-bearers in front.

When a narrow fold of the hillside made it necessary for the procession to swing over to the right, it was now possible to make out in the flicker of the torches some of the people in front.

Nicodemus clutched Joseph's arm, and without slowing his pace pointed to the lean, cloaked figure leading the lot of them. "There goes the man I spoke about!" he said, short of breath with hurrying. "That's one of his own disciples!"

"Judas?"

"Aye, Judas Iscariot, I believe. And he seems to know exactly where to lead them."

But Joseph had noticed something else, and what he saw produced an instant intake of breath. Walking just a pace behind the High Priest Caiaphas and his servant was Joseph's foster father, Malachi, with Mordecai the Suffragan on one side of him and some of the other elders on the other.

That his father should have stooped to lend his presence to this nocturnal trickery seemed scarcely credible, for Malachi had ever been so scrupulous and honorable. To pander visibly to the scheme of some renegade disciple was so unlike him that Joseph stared hard, trying to convince himself that what he saw was actually happening.

It was no hallucination, however, even though the smokey flicker of the torches did indeed give the scene some of the wildness of a dream.

MAN BEFORE THE MORNING

The crowd around them now was the kind of mob that thirsted for excitement—the riffraff of Jerusalem, the let's-go-where-the-trouble-is herd. And in the windless night they carried their arid, animal smell around with them.

Their chatter ranged from undisguised bloodthirstiness to sanctimonious prattle about the need to purify the land of troublemakers. The poison of it all was like an evil current flowing into what Joseph had always felt before was one of the quietest and most restful spots outside the city walls.

He knew that he must keep his head, but he also knew that taking a stand might be inevitable. And he would have to speak his mind no matter what the cost might be.

It was then that he saw the other group emerging from the shadow of the trees.

Despite the sharpness of the moonlight, it was not easy at first to identify the figures in that group, but obviously they had seen the oncoming mob. Soon Joseph realized that the man who led them was Jesus himself.

The two groups neared each other, and as they did so a strange and burdened silence fell upon them all. It was deep and tenacious, a silence that neither Joseph nor Nicodemus could find words to break.

It was the voice of Judas that shattered the silence. Turning to the officer in charge of the soldiers just behind him, and to the chief priests and the elders, he said quite clearly, "The one I kiss is your man; seize him!"

Then Judas stepped quite boldly toward Jesus, and with a loud, "Hail, Rabbi!" kissed him on the cheek.

Standing in the stillness Jesus said simply, "Friend, what are you here for?"

It seemed to Joseph, listening with the rest, that the small word "friend" stood out above the others. It grew upon him that there was no anger or bitterness in it, even though it must have been so mercilessly clear what Judas purposed by this time.

Judas gave no reply. Instead he looked away, with an oddly mask-like face, toward the Captain of the Guard. And as if this were a prearranged signal, the officer ordered his men forward.

As they closed on Jesus all was pandemonium, but despite the din that broke out all about him the words of Jesus could even yet be heard for a moment or so above the noise. "Do you take me for a thief that you have come with swords and cudgels to arrest me? Day after day when I was in the Temple with you, you kept your hands off me. But this is your moment and the power of darkness!"

One of his closest followers shouted out, "Lord, shall we use our swords?" and even before the words were uttered fighting broke sharply out among them. When

MAN BEFORE THE MORNING

Malchus, the High Priest's servant, raised his cudgel over Jesus—Joseph thought it must have been to protect the Nazarene rather than to attack him—another of the disciples did indeed draw his sword, flashing it down upon Malchus' head and cutting through his ear.

Once again above the frenzy of the crowd the voice of the Galilean rang out, "Put up your sword! All who take the sword die by the sword!" And Joseph watched as Jesus touched the head of the screaming Malchus and healed him. In shock the servant woodenly put his hand to his head and realized what had happened. In wonder he knelt there in the midst of all the tumult to stare into the Master's face, until the milling crowd had knocked him sideways and surged across him, leaving him at length to struggle to his feet as best he could.

Joseph leaped forward, yelling for all to desist, but was drowned out in the roar. Nicodemus tried to restrain him by putting a hand on his shoulder. Then as Joseph turned he was knocked down by a man stumbling backward.

On his knees Joseph saw Jesus try to calm the crowd and restrain his disciples. And with a stab of pain and wonder he saw that for a moment the eyes of Jesus were gazing across the intervening space directly at him.

There seemed to be some mystery of recognition in them, and once again there was the indescribable conviction that Joseph had known once before when he was in the Temple. It was as if a quiet voice had once again said,

MAN BEFORE THE MORNING

"I'm going to need you!" And then the commanding eyes turned elsewhere, but not before Joseph had whispered, "And I will *meet* your need, whatever it might be!"

The multitude began to shout more loudly, with such a hubbub centering round Jesus as they seized him that no man could distinctly hear what any other man was saying.

In this swaying crowd, Joseph abruptly struggled to his feet only to realize that Nicodemus was no longer with him. He began to cry out to the people about this crime taking place before their eyes.

"Listen to me!" he shouted; then more loudly, "Listen to me!"

They did not seem to hear him. "Hear me!" he shouted again. "They have no right to seize this man, as they have done, without a charge. They have no right to lead him off in chains like this!"

No one even tried to listen. All were shouting. Some were crying out in pain or fear, some were cursing, some were appealing for mercy. Stung by the wild futility of it, Joseph shouted all the more, "Listen! For God's sake listen to me! I am a Scribe, I tell you. I am of the Council of the Sanhedrin!"

At last the magic word appeared to turn the attention of a few who were closest to him. "I know what I'm talking about!" Joseph went on. "Those who permit this thing are breaking the Law themselves!"

He stopped there, realizing with a physical shock that

147

the only man who was really listening, the only man who had stopped to listen, was his foster father, Malachi. And Malachi was white with anger.

"Fool, thank God they cannot hear you! The Lord be thanked Drusilla cannot hear you either! You must be possessed."

Joseph stared back at his father, meeting the challenge head on. There could be no turning back now and he knew it. "I've only just begun to find my reason, Father. All the cant you have allowed to fester round you has robbed you of your power to see what's right or wrong at last!"

"Are you for this criminal?"

Joseph stared at this man to whom he owed so much, this man he had learned to respect and love as a father. There was a fearful pause, and then he gave his answer sharply and finally: "I am for Jesus."

"Son! You don't know what you're saying!"

"I said I am for Jesus. And I mean that, even if I have to fight for him against you, Father. Even if I have to proclaim the Law itself against you and the Council!"

"You will hold your peace, Joseph!"

Joseph looked wildly round about him. No others had, it seemed, so much as paused to hear them. The man Jesus and his guards, the priests, the Elders, the mob—all were now disappearing through the furthermost belt of trees and would any moment now emerge upon the road into Jerusalem.

Joseph turned from Malachi without another word and ran headlong after the man whose cause he had proclaimed his own.

But two other pairs of eyes had been watching him. Two other pairs of ears had heard what they had hoped to hear.

In the shadow of an olive tree Zibeon gave a quick sign to his companion, and Ephraim, hurrying to overtake two men with cudgels who appeared to be hanging back for him on the fringe of the moving crowd, passed to them the words that Zibeon had spoken.

Of these things Joseph knew nothing. He had now reached the maze of narrow streets at the outskirts of the city. Finally he had worked his way to the head of the procession on the right, but as he turned a corner a hand was clapped across his mouth from behind. He tried to defend himself. He tried to shout; he tried to breathe as he was pulled then dragged into an alleyway. He could not even turn to catch a glimpse of his assailants.

Next he felt a sharp blow on his head, and another, enough to send him reeling down onto the cobblestones. He struck out blindly but another blow, more violent and sickening than the others, brought with it a wild and agonizing surge of pain.

All of a sudden he was back in the caravan again. The thieves were upon him. He saw his mother and father go down under the swords of the thieves. Then they surged over him like a wave of evil. And the terror and hopelessness he had kept locked inside him for years burst forth. Now all was lost—his life, Drusilla and his Lord. And oblivion swallowed him up.

CHAPTER

7

The whole of a long night and part of yet another day had passed before the man from Arimathea began to be aware of things around him.

What he first saw was a flickering candle on a single candlestick. It stood upon a narrow table pushed against the wall just opposite the plain, long bed in which he now found himself.

He put his hand up to his head, as if to fend away the pain that lingered there. Then as he raised himself to lean upon one elbow he realized that he was not alone in the room.

An aged woman sitting by the small window rose and came across to him, the candlelight softening the smile with which she looked down at him.

"I am glad, master," she said, "to see that you can move again. My son and I had wondered if you ever would."

He looked down at the plain brown tunic he wore —and she nodded at him as if anticipating his question. "Yes, it is not your robe, master. I had to wash the bloodstains from your clothes, sir, and my son Zophar and I helped you into one of his tunics until your own clothes were dry and clean again. How grateful I am to see you waking up at last!"

He stared about him in astonishment.

"Where am I?" he asked.

"You are in the house of Zophar the potter, sir, on the road back from Gethsemane into Jerusalem."

"How did I get here, then?"

"My son and I went to the door to see the crowds that were surging by last night, and we found you lying unconscious and badly beaten. We brought you back in here to see how best we could help you."

"May God be praised and bless you, woman! And what is your name, pray?"

"I am Sarah."

"Then thank you, Sarah!"

Joseph looked about him, seeing at the window something that surprised him.

"Surely I have not been here two nights already, Sarah?"

MAN BEFORE THE MORNING

She shook her head at that. "No, sir. It is still quite early on the morning after you were attacked. You slept—or were unconscious—all through the night. This morning. . . ."

"Morning? Why then is it still so dark out there?"

They both looked into the eerie darkness that was beyond the window. It seemed to be the black of night yet it was not night. It was not a mist or fog or cloud; rather it seemed an all-enveloping shadow, muffling not only light but in some strange and frightening way silencing all sound as well.

Without looking back directly at him, Sarah said, "The soothsayers are declaring that the darkness has to do with this Nazarene who has been crucified on Golgotha!"

"Did you say, 'has *been* crucified,' woman?"

"Yes, master."

The words hit him with all the intensity of another blow from a club. Crucified! He was too late! Jesus could never heal Drusilla now! He tried to swing himself out of the bed, but could not. He fell back for a moment exhausted, drained not only physically by his injuries but emotionally as well by the news he had just heard.

But he had to hear more. Turning to Sarah once again he said, "Tell me everything you know about the crucifixion."

Sarah seemed afraid of the question.

Looking more closely across at her, and speaking more gently, Joseph said, "You do not need to be afraid of telling me about this thing, Sarah."

Almost in a whisper she said, "You are of the Sanhedrin, my Lord."

"Does that make you afraid of me?" he asked.

She did not answer directly. Instead she said, "My son Zophar is a friend of Shuah, himself a servant of yet another Councillor of the Sanhedrin."

"I know this Shuah, Sarah. He is the servant of a good friend of mine, called Nicodemus."

She seemed to lose much of her fear when she heard him confirm what Shuah had already told her. "Nicodemus is a friend of yours?" she asked.

Joseph smiled at her. "My friend Nicodemus, like myself, is in the Sanhedrin but increasingly not of the Sanhedrin. But I have not told you my own name, Sarah. I am Joseph of Arimathea."

She nodded at him. "This we already know, sir. Shuah came last night while you were lying there unconscious and he recognized you. He wanted to carry you straightway to the house of his master, Nicodemus—but Zophar and I believed it better that you should lie here safely, at least until you could talk again."

"But what of Nicodemus?"

"He too, master, has not been home. My son Zophar and

Shuah are now out looking for him. They could come back at any moment."

He stared at her for a moment, then asked the most important question of all. He asked it quietly, despite the tenseness that had been growing about him in these last few months.

"Sarah, are you and your son—are you believers in this Jesus?"

For a second or two she gazed back at him, and the flicker of the candle seemed to intensify her reply.

"Yes, master."

After another moment of silence he said—and this too was almost in a whisper—"Then God has indeed been gracious to me, Sarah! How else could those who attacked me have left me at your doorstep? You see, I too want to follow Jesus."

"But he has been crucified!"

"I don't know how to explain it, Sarah, but I believe this is not the end..."

He did not finish what he was about to say, for the door from the street opened now and two men came hurrying into the house.

Joseph tried to stand but the weakness of his legs made him fall back upon the bed again. He made another attempt, however, and this time slowly stood erect.

One of the men was Shuah, who was quick to recognize

Joseph, noting the plain brown tunic instead of the richer robe that he had worn last night. The other man was younger, a thick-set man who looked at Joseph with a touch of awkwardness.

Sarah was quick to explain; turning to Joseph she said, "This is my son, Zophar the potter, sir."

Zophar said to his mother. "We have found my lord Nicodemus, Mother!" He then turned to Joseph and said, "He waits for you, my lord Joseph of Arimathea, at the foot of the cross on Golgotha. That is, of course, if you can yet walk that far."

"I can indeed walk that far," said Joseph simply.

Sarah interrupted this with a gentle, "There is milk here, sir, that you should drink and a little bread and honey before you go. It'll give you strength."

Joseph was grateful. "I'll drink the milk, Sarah, but I'll not need the rest."

She nodded, bringing back Joseph's own robe that had been washed and dried for him from the other end of the room. This she gave to him, and while he put it on she went back to the far shelf again to bring him a small pitcher of milk and a drinking cup.

Impatient to be gone again, Shuah said to Joseph, "My master said I was to tell you that Jesus is not yet dead. He asked that you please hurry, if you could."

Wearing his own familiar robe again, Joseph took the milk from Sarah hurriedly but gratefully.

MAN BEFORE THE MORNING

Then, leaving Zophar with his mother, the two of them went out into the darkness of the street outside.

* * * *

The journey to Golgotha was not a long one. Despite the savagery of the attack from which he had been rescued by Zophar, Joseph found growing strength in the very urgency of the situation.

Crowds of people seemed to be coming back from Golgotha, and were moving slowly along the road to the city in the half light. Joseph feared that it might be all over—that he was too late.

The thoughtful Shuah had stretched out an arm for Joseph to lean upon, and the man from Arimathea was grateful for the support. It could not be over! It could not! Something was yet to come, he felt sure.

For a little while there was a burdened silence between them, but for Joseph the silence was filled with two searing anxieties. One was the spectacle which he knew awaited him on Golgotha. The other was his desperate concern about Drusilla. Even in this strange twilight and dead silence that surrounded them, Joseph kept hearing in his head the promise he had made her not to return until he had found his peace about Jesus.

More and more he had realized how much it must have cost his wife—lying as she was herself upon the edge of death—to urge this promise on him. She had been urging him to choose life. Not to be lost in her death but to choose the Master he would serve—for life.

They came at last over the brow of a small rise of land and saw on the other side of a shallow valley the hill called Golgotha.

The shadowy dark around them was not too deep to see the three gaunt crosses on the top of it. Nor could they fail to see the men nailed to them, and the two soldiers—one of them a Centurion—who stood near the crosses, evidently placed on guard there.

There was a wind across this place. It was an eerie, unfamiliar sound, because there were no trees to either muffle or mold it. And in some strange way the moaning of this wind appeared to be a part of the general darkness that covered the scene.

But it was toward the figure on the central cross and the people who stood about the foot of it that Joseph and Shuah now made their way.

There were some womenfolk there. One of them—perhaps the oldest—was leaning against the shoulder of a younger man. And not too far away from them Joseph beheld with quick relief the figure of Nicodemus.

Nicodemus saw his colleague at the same time, and came toward him. As they met Nicodemus began to speak about the happenings that had separated them and had led him to this place, but Joseph felt a sudden need to

158

stand quite still, to lift his eyes and look into the face of Jesus. There would be time among themselves—yes, endless time—for explanations later. But first they must look with special tenderness upon this man whose presence in this place had drawn them here, who seemingly powerless and dying they had come to serve.

They stood in silence, gazing up at him and realizing that the darkness that covered everything else did not seem to cover him completely, but left a brightness about his head and on the superscription that had been placed upon the cross above him. It read: THE KING OF THE JEWS.

There was no sound or word from the two malefactors on either side of him, though one of them appeared to turn his head from time to time, despite the agony this would cause.

Neither Nicodemus nor Joseph had been able to speak to each other as they stood there, until Joseph with grief and conflict in his voice said in a whisper to his friend, "Who are the others, Nicodemus? Where are his closest friends? Where are his disciples? How could they leave him in this fashion?"

It seemed as if this simple questioning opened in Joseph's heart a flood of terrible misgivings, and a sudden surge of doubt.

He had asked himself, "What if the teachings of this man were of the moment only? What if his doctrine in these precious years has been but a matter of mere words? What if the faith he has proclaimed is but a hollow faith? Not even his disciples are at hand that we might question them about his prophecies. . . ."

Joseph lowered his head and clenched his fingers in an agony of tension. He was, he told himself, of the Sanhedrin itself—he belonged to the group of men who had crucified this man. Yet no one but Nicodemus had sought Jesus out to talk alone with him.

Joseph thrust these dark thoughts sharply from his mind as he stood there.

Jesus was still alive. He looked steadily down upon the little group gathered there, particularly at the older woman who, Joseph concluded, must be his mother. Indeed even as Joseph watched and listened, she looked at Jesus with all the earnestness of measureless compassion, saying simply in deep grief, yet loudly enough for Joseph to hear, "My son . . . My son!"

For a moment Joseph could not bear to look at her and turned away, but as he looked back upon that central cross again he saw that the Nazarene was looking down at him.

Not a word was spoken. Yet in those deep, afflicted eyes Joseph saw a moment's recognition. And, despite the agony through which this man was passing, there was not only love but the same unvoiced commandment that had impressed Joseph in the Temple. Then suddenly the pat-

160

tern God had made unfolded before him. He is dying, Joseph thought, dying. Alone. He was homeless while he lived, but he will have a place in death. He will not be abandoned like a criminal. I have a tomb prepared, and I will obey God's command.

It was with love that Joseph looked up in silence at his Lord. It was a purer love than the man from Arimathea had ever known or shown. And as he, too, gazed up at the figure on the cross, he made a silent pledge to Jesus that he would carry out those orders or events. He would obey them, wherever they might lead him, and whatever they might entail.

In the silence around the central cross the wind was rising. It almost seemed to be a great, vast sighing for the world, a rising and falling of the spirit that sought to shatter all that still seemed holy in the scene. Then even the wind itself appeared to pause around them, and the voice of Jesus spoke in sudden clarity, a cry filled with its own despair.

"Eloi, Eloi, lama sabachthani? My God, my God, why have you forsaken me?"

Joseph of Arimathea closed his eyes tightly for a moment, no longer able to look up into that face. He told himself that those few words were not destroying the faith that was in him.

Joseph opened his eyes again to see one of the young men who stood by the cross on the other side of Mary run to fill a sponge with sour wine. He put it on a reed and with compassion raised it to Jesus' lips, but Jesus turned away. He didn't need it now.

Instead, above the sighing of the wind that rose around him, he lifted his head and spoke once more.

"Father," he said, "into your hands I commit my spirit."

And at last his head fell forward. And Joseph knew, as he heard these words, that the terrifying doubt was over. Jesus would again be with his Father.

It was over.

His mother gasped and broke into a series of heart-rending sobs. The others were heartbroken but silent and for a moment there was no movement. Then suddenly a great rumble of thunder or a shaking in the earth startled them.

As the last sounds faded away Joseph walked across to the mother of Jesus. "Dear lady," he said, as quietly as the wind which also seemed to die about them now.

Mary looked anxiously at the man who now approached her and at the older man who followed modestly after him but stayed some little distance behind.

"Dear lady," Joseph said again, "My name is Joseph, and I am from Arimathea. I have been asking myself what I could do for you, and"—glancing up at the cross behind him—"for him."

The disciple with Mary listened to Joseph with some suspicion. It was with grief rather than with fear or anger, however, that he said, "Is it not too late now to ask what you can do?"

"No. I feel that it is not too late, for me at least, to render some small service—and to demonstrate the love I had no opportunity to show him while he lived. I believe that I was given an answer to my prayer."

Jesus' mother looked at him inquiringly. "What do you mean?" she asked.

With deep compassion Joseph said, "Out on the hillside, lady, I have a newly made sepulchre. I believe it is God's plan that I should offer it to your son."

"Would the authorities let you do this?"

"I'll go at once to Pontius Pilate and request the body of the Lord."

Mary seemed to notice for the first time the richness of Joseph's robe, and apprehension grew in her eyes at what she imagined. "What have you to do with Pontius Pilate?" she asked anxiously.

For a moment Joseph stood silently, an emotional warfare going on inside him. He realized that there was nothing he could do now but tell her the truth. He would have to confess himself a believer, if not to the son, then to the mother.

"I belong to the Council of the Sanhedrin," he said simply, "but in most matters that concern them, I am a man apart. And concerning your son, dear lady, I have almost ceased to be a member of the Sanhedrin and so has my good friend Nicodemus. For your son we have both become outcasts—willingly, gratefully." He stretched his hand toward Nicodemus, and the older man approached them.

"Nicodemus will tell you," Joseph went on, "that both of us tried to prevent the Sanhedrin from acting as it did. Yet because of hatred, anger and jealousy among them, they moved too quickly for us."

Again the young disciple asked, "What good is this information to us now?" And Joseph, stretching out his hands in yet more earnest pleading toward the sorrowing Mary, said again, "Once the Council of the Sanhedrin knows that we too are followers of your son, our work within the Council will be over. For that matter, even our lives may be in danger, Yet with all my heart I wish to give the body of your son the safety and security of my own tomb.

The deep anxiety in Mary's eyes was replaced now by a new thankfulness. "It may be hard to get permission for such a thing," she said.

Joseph nodded his agreement. "The Roman law," he said, "is not equipped for such a gift. It is to the Romans that his body now belongs to do with as they wish—even to leave him there."

Mary wept openly again, putting her small, pale hands up to her eyes as if she could no longer look upon this scene.

164

MAN BEFORE THE MORNING

The young man beside her said, "I am his follower, John. I'll take Mary home with me; indeed, the Lord made it one of his last requests that I treat her as my own mother. I'll take good care of her. We deeply appreciate what you propose to do."

"And I will go to Pilate at once," Joseph said, "leaving my friend Nicodemus to stand watch until I return again—speedily, I hope—with Pilate's permission. Pray for me and pray that I will be successful."

Mary lifted a hand in an acknowledgement of his words and in a silent benediction then turned away with John. "That I shall do, Joseph!" she said, "and I shall pray for Nicodemus also."

CHAPTER
8

For a moment or so Pontius Pilate sat silently in the audience chamber of the praetorium—the Herodian palace he used as a residence at times such as the Jewish Passover. And although for a brief space of time he sat in silence, he seemed strangely ill-at-ease as he waited there.

He was seated on a dais, raised a few steps above the floor of the hall. The marble throne on which he sat was flanked by two tall pedestal braziers. Both of these braziers were now lit, and the flicker of their flames gave a curious air of restlessness to the scene—a restlessness that seemed intensified by the rich and heavy hangings that covered the wall in the background.

In this luxurious and austere setting, the Procurator leaned back against the fur skins draped over the marble

167

seat. One thin hand stretched out from his toga to tap restlessly on the arm of the seat. He was a strong man, one obviously used to command. Yet, like many Romans born to power, he had a somewhat effete air about him and a weakening of moral fibre.

A young man, one of his personal servants, clad in a brief tunic, stood at his side quite motionless. And both of them listened sharply to the sound of footsteps advancing over the marble floor.

It was another servant who approached now, leading the dignified figure of Joseph across the room.

Reaching the foot of the throne, the servant said simply: "Excellency, I bring to you my lord Joseph, of the Sanhedrin." He bowed deeply to the Procurator and withdrew.

Joseph bowed more deeply to Pilate and Pilate returned it with an almost expressionless nod of recognition. Then he said with a touch of sarcasm in his voice, "I'd hoped the Sanhedrin might have given me some rest. Getting its own way about things is developing into quite a habit, don't you think?"

"Doesn't that rather depend on what you consider to be their own way, Excellency?"

"I could give you quite a list of things that would fit well into that category." He looked as if he were about to list these items as they came to him, but he stared for a moment or so at Joseph. Here, he thought, is a dignified, respectful young man from the Sanhedrin. Joseph projected an air almost of supplication which Pilate found more appropriate than the presumption of most men from that body. So Pilate decided to deal directly with the matter now at hand.

"The scribe you sent ahead of you to ask permission for this interview declared that you considered what you had to talk about to be a matter of some urgency."

"I would indeed so look upon it, sir."

Pilate clasped his long, thin hands and settled back as if he were about to listen to and then perhaps indulge some worthless whim.

"What is it, Councillor?" he asked.

Joseph glanced with momentary uneasiness at the servant standing beside Pilate, then back at the Procurator again. He forced himself to rise entirely above his fears in this situation.

Calmly and earnestly he looked at the man who sat upon the throne, and spoke more fearlessly than he had expected to.

"I came, sir, to beg the body of the man Jesus of Nazareth who was crucified today."

Pilate looked up at the reflected flicker of the braziers on the ceiling. Half to himself he said, as if afflicted by the memory, "King of the Jews!"

Joseph said calmly, "I came to beg his body for burial, sir. I have a garden close to Golgotha. And in it is a newly-finished sepulchre."

Pilate had sat more upright at the news. He looked at Joseph with surprise. "And you would lay a stranger in this tomb of yours?" he asked.

"Yes, sir," replied Joseph.

The Procurator tried to sit back more casually against his throne. Dropping his voice a little he asked, "Are you then a follower of this man?"

"I am, sir."

"You are, then—or should I say more rightly that you were—a disciple of that poor, deserted Galilean?"

Joseph said simply, "I came to beg his body for burial, sir."

Pilate shrugged his shoulders imcomprehensively.

"I doubt he's even dead yet, Joseph."

"I have just come from Golgotha, sir. I stood beneath the cross in this curious darkness as did some others.

"Is it still dark outside?"

"I think the dark was lifting as I came away, sir—as if the thing were over now. I heard the last words that he spoke, sir, and watched his head fall on his chest.

"And then?"

Joseph looked at Pilate with a totally unexpected new awareness of deep concern. His own words rose to meet that question with a strange new depth of fellow-feeling. "It seemed as if there were a rolling of deep thunder in the earth, sir. I don't think any man is likely to forget it. It shook the ground we stood upon, so that we all drew closer to each other until the rumble rolled away into the hills."

Pilate had placed his hands over his eyes as though he did not wish to see what he was imagining. Then he leaned forward to speak to Joseph more quietly and earnestly. Suddenly he wanted to bridge the gap between them. "Today," he said, "has been too full of mysteries. This Jesus said to me, before they took him off, he said ... 'For this cause came I into the world, that I should bear witness unto the truth.' I am not likely to forget the way he said it."

"I can so well believe that, sir."

The Procurator seemed to try to brush aside whatever thoughts were troubling him, and spoke to Joseph with more emphasis and loudly. "I'm still not sure he's dead," he said. "I shall find out for you." And so saying he turned to the young servant at his side.

"The Centurion in charge of the crucifixion party should be back by now, Malchus. Go to the gatehouse and see if he's there. If so, beg him come here to me. You needn't return until I send for you. You understand?"

"Yes, Excellency." The young man bowed quickly and

withdrew. Pilate watched him go, and once he was quite sure they were alone again, he said more confidentially, "There is a warning I must give you, Councillor."

Joseph raised his eyebrows a little. "A warning, sir?" he said.

Pilate nodded and seemed more at ease once again.

"I've known about you long enough, Joseph of Arimathea, to realize how highly your place is valued in the Sanhedrin. I know the kind of brilliant future they expect to be lying ahead for you there. I know you have enemies—so why, Joseph ... why end your chances by espousing a lost cause like this? What possible good could you do to this Jesus of Nazareth now?"

Joseph did not flinch at the words.

"I only know that I have come to believe in him, sir, and in the things he taught."

Pilate shook his head uncomprehendingly. "A young man doing so well in the Sanhedrin," he said, "might well consider if he wants to throw away a whole career for a mere religious whim. The greater your standing, the greater the envy it arouses, I know. I speak from deep experience. This will be used against you."

"I'm well aware of that, sir."

"Then move with caution ... as I try to do myself!"

Joseph was silent, and Pilate went on talking. "You know what the Sanhedrin might do to you officially as a follower of this Nazarene? Do you know what they might seek to do to you more unofficially?"

"I have already had some evidence of that, sir. And yet, I'm doing what I have to do."

"And yet you come to me like this? You come admitting that you are his follower even after his death?"

They both looked up at the sound of footsteps nearing them across the floor. Pilate said no more, letting a shrug of the shoulders convey the futility and stupidity he felt and nodding in the direction of the arm extended in salute by the Centurion who now approached him.

"You're just back from the crucifixion on Golgotha, Quartus?"

"Yes, Excellency."

"I'm told this Nazarene's already dead up there upon the cross. It doesn't seem very likely."

"It's true, sir."

"How do you know this?"

"One of the guards pierced his side with his lance, sir, and water and blood flowed out."

Quite suddenly the Centurion seemed to remember this spectacle only too vividly and almost shuddered. He tried to conceal his feelings by dropping his head to stare only at the floor.

The Procurator watched with deep astonishment.

"Come now, Quartus," he said, "you've captained many a crucifixion party. It's not for you to seem so troubled a man!"

The Centurion looked up from the floor again but this clearly was not easy for him. After a significant pause he said with an unwonted quietness, "This was no ordinary man, sir."

"Speak up, Quartus," Pilate said. "I cannot hear you."

Clearly and loudly the Centurion said, "This was no ordinary man, Excellency. It was an *evil* thing we did up there!"

Pilate looked sharply at the man, showing perhaps some inner sense of torment at the words.

"You were not asked for any comment!" he said sharply. Then turning to Joseph again he said with chagrin and finality, "You have my permission to take him away, Councillor. And bury him. Aye, *bury him!*"

Joseph bowed briefly. "Thank you, sir," he said.

Then Pilate turned again to the Centurion. "Take this Rabbi back to Golgotha, Quartus. Give him all the help you can with the body of this Nazarene."

"Yes, sir." The Centurion saluted again. Joseph bowed once more to the Procurator, then went out from his presence at the side of the Centurion.

And as they left the audience chamber both of them heard the voice of Pilate, repeating almost deliriously to himself: "This was no ordinary man, it seems. *This was no ordinary man!*"

CHAPTER
9

It was already late afternoon by the time Joseph and Nicodemus had laid the body of Jesus upon the ledge of rock within the hand-hewn sepulchre.

The fact that Joseph had purchased the tomb for his own family was no longer of any moment. What mattered most was that at long last after the agony of Golgotha the body of the Lord was resting in peace in a proper place that Joseph had sought so earnestly to provide.

This was a quiet place, a refuge from the crowd and from the imprecations of so many in that crowd. It was indeed so silent in the sepulchre that now and then they could even hear the singing of the birds in the garden outside.

The two friends spoke in whispers for each of them

now felt—without voicing the thought—that in some way this place had become a holy sanctuary.

Nicodemus had brought with him a generous supply of myrrh and aloes with which to anoint the body of Jesus, and he set quickly about his task with tenderness and reverence.

"Is it not strange," said Joseph, "that as yet none of his followers have sought to see him? It would indeed seem that they had deserted him."

Nicodemus shook his head. "Mary," he said, "asked to come with the disciple John to see the sepulchre while you were closeted with Pilate—even before we knew that he would agree to your request."

"I wish I had seen her."

"She was much stricken with grief. Yet when she told me of the gratitude she felt that you had offered such a tomb, she spoke with strange tranquility."

"God bless her, Nicodemus!"

Nicodemus paused a moment. "He may have blessed her more than any of us will ever know, Joseph. As to the sepulchre, she knew, I think, that it could not have been an easy task for you to seek out Pilate."

Joseph nodded, unfolding the linen shroud that he had brought with him. "It wasn't easy, Nicodemus."

The older man did not look up again as he said, "I think Pilate must have felt guilt or at least uncertainty about what has happened. Perhaps it eased his conscience to give you what you asked for."

MAN BEFORE THE MORNING

"He didn't seem unwilling, Nicodemus. And he did indeed look like a man on the edge of torment."

Joseph folded back the shroud where such a fold was called for. After a moment he looked around him and said, "Yes, the edge of torment. That's where I've been too. Its has been three long days now since Drusilla and I saw one another!

"Every hour within those days I have prayed and prayed and prayed for her, Nicodemus. There have been times when I have longed to flee this tragedy on Calvary and get back to Arimathea."

Nicodemus said quietly, "I know how hard that must have been for you, my friend."

Joseph continued: "Yet what was happening to this Nazarene seemed stronger and more vital to me than anything else. Did I tell you it was Drusilla herself who urged me to make my peace with Jesus before I returned to her? She hadn't even seen him, Nicodemus, but in her heart of hearts she knew I was ready to follow him. Her words come singing back to me as I think of them. 'Promise that you won't come back to me,' she said, 'before you've either found him or found peace about him!'"

Nicodemus looked earnestly at his suffering friend. "I too have prayed for Drusilla," he said. "I wonder what she would think of the future that must face us now?"

For just a moment Joseph raised his eyes above the linen shroud and looked at Nicodemus closely.

MAN BEFORE THE MORNING

"For Drusilla," he said, "there is no future now. Yet once she is aware of what's happened here, I think she'll know, even with her Sadducean upbringing, that we have acted in the only way our consciences would let us act. And I think she would approve."

Joseph resumed his work with the linen under his fingers, and Nicodemus bent over the precious ointments again.

"Sooner or later, Joseph, we would have left the Council of the Sanhedrin. Neither of us could act out a part we no longer believed in. Nor could we expect them to keep us in their company. Friends of a crucified felon have no place in such an august and righteous body as the Sanhedrin. Not when even his own followers have deserted or abandoned him!" Nicodemus said.

Joseph shook his head at that.

"It's ironic but even as I look about this tomb I have a feeling that we're not so much a part of an ending as of a beginning! I think. . . ." He stopped there, hearing someone approaching the entrance to the sepulchre.

There were two women's voices. The voices fell silent at the threshold of the tomb.

Joseph stood upright and went toward the rounded, rough-hewn door, stooping to step out. There he stood on a level with the two women who now awaited him. Nicodemus, still busy with the spices he had brought, remained in the sepulchre behind him.

MAN BEFORE THE MORNING

The older woman, holding against her robe a little alabaster box of precious ointment, looked at Joseph with some anxiety, but with respect.

"You are my lord Joseph of Arimathea?" she asked.

"I am," he said, and returned her gaze with a little nod of reassurance.

"It was the Centurion who has been placed on guard out there," she said, "who gave us your name, sir. He said you were the owner of this tomb, and that the Rabbi Nicodemus was also with you."

"Yes, lady. He is finishing the anointing while he still may. I see you have a little vessel of precious ointment with you, lady."

"It's spikenard. I didn't tell you my name, sir. I am Mary, the wife of Cleophas. And this is Mary of Magdala."

The younger woman bowed to him respectfully, as one would bow to a ruler of the Jews. She was a woman of great beauty, though her eyes now bore the marks of bitter weeping.

"I had to come, sir, before the tomb was sealed," she said. "I owe my very life to him. He had so much love and compassion to share with us all!"

Joseph smiled kindly at her as she stood there.

"There is still time, Mary of Magdala," he said gently. "Go in to Nicodemus and take the spikenard with you."

She took the jar of ointment from her companion, and as Joseph stood aside to let her pass her saffron robe so gently brushed him and something of the sweet scent of the ointment wafted by.

To the older woman he said, "I'm glad you came in time, wife of Cleophas. Soon it will be the Sabbath, and the tomb must be sealed by then."

The woman said fervently, "Those of us who followed Jesus will be ever grateful to you for giving him your own sepulchre, sir!" And then almost in a whisper she added, "None of us thought you would dare reveal yourself as one of his followers! Especially when it was all over, sir!"

Mary of Magdala, now within the sepulchre, had heard these last few words. "I know how dangerous such a step must have been!" she said. "But he would bless you for it!"

Joseph turned to look at her, and even in the shadow of the tomb there seemed to be some light of wonder in her face. "Simon Peter," she said, "has reminded us of what Jesus said to the disciples just last week!"

"What did he say?"

"When they were coming with him into Jerusalem, and some of them were concerned about his safety, he said 'Behold, we go up to Jerusalem; and the Son of Man shall be delivered unto the chief priests and unto the scribes, and they shall condemn him to death ... and they shall mock him and shall scourge him, and spit upon him, and shall kill him; *and the third day he shall rise again.*'"

"I did not hear this."

MAN BEFORE THE MORNING

"I pray," she said, "that those words are true! And oh, my lord Joseph, how much you have honored him!"

Joseph remembered, as she spoke, the look that had passed between him and Jesus as he hung dying on his cross. And yet he did not dare speak of such a thing. There was some special glory in it that held him silent.

For a little while longer the sepulchre was quiet. Then Joseph spoke again.

"Mary of Magdala," he said, "if you want to use that spikenard you brought with you, I beg you finish with it quickly. All of us must soon leave this place until the Sabbath is over. Nicodemus and I will be rolling the heavy stone across the entrance to seal the tomb. We can come again later if some of his followers want to see him for the last time."

Joseph waited outside the tomb for the others. The western sky was aflame as the sun set and he thought of Drusilla once again.

And with his face turned northwest toward Arimathea, he whispered, "I shall be with you soon, Drusilla, my love, and every moment until then I shall be praying for you!"

CHAPTER
10

Joseph and Nicodemus spent a quiet and sorrowful Passover in the latter's house. When the sunset ended the day of rest, they waited only until the moon rose before setting out on the journey. They rode as quickly as possible through the night, stopping only to rest their horses. It was a great relief to Joseph to recognize at last, even in the darkness, the familiar curve of road that would take him directly to his home.

Nicodemus had come with him on this journey to seek a place of peace away from the Sanhedrin, a place where the two of them might do all that could be done for Drusilla and where they could talk about their plans for the future.

Both of them knew that Joseph's foster father, Malachi,

183

would almost certainly not be in Arimathea. An emergency meeting of the Sanhedrin had been called in Jerusalem and Malachi was not likely to be absent from it.

Joseph was glad to have the company of his friend, and he was grateful that in the early dark like this it was easy to talk together privately as they moved.

Looking straight ahead Nicodemus said, "I have been praying that we will find Drusilla well."

Joseph nodded gratefully, glad to have the company of this older friend, thankful to have the wisdom of those extra years beside him now.

"If I'm to believe Sosthenes," he said, "then I must realize that every day that passes might well be her last, Nicodemus. I'm grateful for your prayers."

They rode in silence. And the words that she had last spoken to him were ringing in his ears again. "I *have* found my peace about him!" he thought. "I knew it when I stood there in the praetorium, face to face with Pilate. I knew it when I looked up at Jesus on his cross, when for that one brief moment he looked at me and I sensed what he wanted me to do. I knew it for certain in the tomb. And what is still more wonderful I know it now. There will be many other things that I can do in his name, things that I can't yet imagine. In that there is peace."

They rode on a while. Then Joseph said, "You know I've never been a prey to idle fancies, friend. And yet I feel as if the world around us almost holds its breath . . . as if some great, momentous thing were readying itself for revelation."

"I think I understand you, Joseph. I have been thinking again of all those things Jesus told me when I went to him one night when my fellow councillors would not see me. One thing stood out above all the others."

"And what was that?"

"He said to me, 'As Moses lifted up the serpent in the wilderness, even so must the Son of Man be lifted up.' I've always wondered what he meant by that. At last I think I know what he meant. I think he spoke of being lifted up upon his cross, Joseph . . . providing a kind of agonized turning point for the world! And yet despite the agony he continued to love all those around him!"

Joseph said quietly, "How can his disciples turn their backs on him, Nicodemus?"

"The people of the world are very stubborn, Joseph. As I look back upon that night I remember another thing he said."

"What?"

"He told me, 'God so loved the world that he gave his only begotten son, that whosoever believeth in him should not perish, but have everlasting life. For God sent not his son into the world to condemn the world, but that the world through him might be saved.' "

MAN BEFORE THE MORNING

Joseph looked wonderingly at his friend and said, "The world!" He had a vision of the earth spread out before him, suffering in bondage, suddenly set free.

They had come around the bend of the hill that led down to the hollow in which Joseph's home was built. And in this darkness there seemed to be an extra silence there.

It was a silence that clutched at Joseph's heart. But Nicodemus seemed to understand and moved in silence at his side.

Coming over the brow of the last small rise of the familiar route Joseph saw his home once again.

He spurred his horse more quickly at the sight, realizing as he did that here and there about the house was an unexpected glow of lamplight.

There was as yet no movement visible around the house, at any rate no movement that could be detected until Joseph was in hailing distance.

Then even though it was still dark, they could dimly see someone come out from the outer courtyard and stand at its entrance holding a lantern. It was Zuilmah.

At the sight of Joseph and his friend she hurried forward, and Joseph dismounted and ran quickly toward her. Nicodemus got off his horse more deliberately and came with it to hold Joseph's mount; he paused a moment, then led both horses into the outer courtyard. He did not hear what Zuilmah had to say to Joseph and yet he

186

sensed it was wiser for him not to hurry as his younger friend had done.

"How is she, Zuilmah?" Joseph asked. He saw the strain of weeping on her face.

"She does not know me, sir. Nor anyone else in the house. She simply lies there with her eyes closed, breathing painfully and stirring not at all, sir. I think ... I think...."

Joseph heard himself say—in a strange and shattering whisper—"You think she's dying?"

Zuilmah could not bring herself to answer. She simply nodded, and half turned to hurry him away into the house.

"Take the Rabbi Nicodemus into the inner courtyard, Zuilmah—and see that he's comfortable until I've seen Drusilla."

"Yes, sir." And she added, "I have sent Jubal back into Jerusalem to tell her father."

Joseph nodded, but was already hurrying past her.

The door to Drusilla's sleeping room was closed. He pushed it open only wide enough to enter, then softly closed it.

In the room there was a single lighted lamp that stood upon a pedestal near her bed. In its light Joseph saw that Drusilla was lying motionless, her arms outside the bedclothes still and white beside her, her head raised up a little by the pillow. He dropped to his knees beside her and leaned forward to kiss her brow.

MAN BEFORE THE MORNING

"Drusilla!" he said. And then more loudly, in a quick new helplessness, "This is Joseph, Drusilla!"

She did not hear him. The fingers of her hand beneath his own were quite cold and still. He tried to give them movement by raising her hand and letting the fingertips rest for a little while upon his lips. He was quite sure she was not conscious of his presence at her side. He placed her hand upon the bedclothes once again but kept his own hand firmly over it.

Drowning out everything else in the room was the painful, strangely loud and echoing sound of her breathing.

He could not take his eyes away from her even a moment. As he knelt there he found that he was repeating the words that Nicodemus had spoken out on the road, "God so loved the world that he gave his only begotten son, that whosoever believeth in him should not perish. . . ."

"Not perish . . . not perish." And as he spoke the words, they lit a hope in him which seemed aflame.

Suddenly he rose to his feet, and with a burning look at Drusilla, rushed to the door and out to speak to Nicodemus. He rushed across the courtyard. Looking beyond its open entrance-way toward a path that led into a garden, he saw the first glow of sunrise beginning to light the sky. He had to see Nicodemus now before it was too late.

MAN BEFORE THE MORNING

Hearing his approach, Nicodemus came to him from the inner courtyard.

"How is she, Joseph?" he asked gently.

Joseph brushed aside the question in his urgency.

"It came to me just now as I sat there, Nicodemus. Tell me again what you said to me on the road ... it started 'God so loved the world....'"

Startled, Nicodemus looked intently at his friend. He feared the worst had happened. "God so loved the world," he said, "that he gave his only begotten son, that whosoever believeth in him should not perish...."

Joseph held up a hand to stop him there. "Nicodemus!" he said, "The promise says, 'Whosoever believeth in him should not perish ... *whosoever believeth in him* ... and, oh, I *do* believe in him! I think that I believe in him enough to prove the meaning of those words ... for words like that belong to all of us; they become the basis for life itself! Pray these words again with me, Nicodemus."

They prayed, Nicodemus at once saddened and joyful for his friend. Joseph was still very agitated so he tried to draw him into conversation. They talked in clear and hopeful tones, their fears forgotten for a while...building their new-born faith together, seeing the truth behind the words they uttered.

Then Nicodemus looked up, his eye catching a slight movement.

MAN BEFORE THE MORNING

"Joseph!" was all he seemed to have the power to say. And Joseph turned to where Nicodemus was staring.

The light heralding the first morning of a new week had begun to reach across the courtyard, and sunlight fell upon the door that Joseph had but lately closed.

And yet that door stood open now. And out of the shadows into the sunlight stepped Drusilla!

Joseph moved toward her, hardly realizing that this was no dream he was seeing. It was no vision he was approaching.

"This is ... a miracle!"

"Joseph, my love," she said, "I do not know how it has come about! I was dreaming. You were in the room. You held my hand. Then you left me. I was so alone. Then someone came. He spoke to me, but I can't remember what he said. He gave me something for you but I don't know what it was. I began to wake ... I felt my strength coming back to me ... I felt well again—*completely* well! I got up and I started to walk...."

Joseph gathered her into his arms, and scarcely heard her say, "Where better could I walk, my love, than into my husband's arms."

Joseph held her from him for a moment, the better to believe what he saw. And then he said, "I thank Almighty God for all of us, Drusilla! I too feel renewed, strengthened. I almost feel as if I were a child again!"

She laughed a little, as if her voice were full of music.

MAN BEFORE THE MORNING

And then, looking beyond him . . . "But I neglect our dear friend Nicodemus!"

The tears were rolling down Nicodemus' cheeks as she came, and he kissed her hand as she reached him, saying, "I, too, thank God for all he has shown us, Drusilla!"

Still amazed Joseph came across to them, and put his arm about his wife once more. "There is so much," he said, "for us to talk about as we wait to see what God has planned for us, Drusilla!"

And then she did a little thing that was so much like the Drusilla of old, the Drusilla he loved so well. She ran a few steps from them, and took a pomegranate blossom from a hedge in the corner of the courtyard. Coming back again she lightly touched it to her lips, then gave it to her husband.

He held it in the palm of his hand almost as if it were a small lamp, yet one that matched the radiance of the morning.

Then all three of them went back into the house together. And the fountain in the courtyard shimmered as they passed and rippled in the light of the new day.